WICKED DAYS

An Ivy Morgan Mystery Book One

LILY HARPER HART

HarperHart Publications

To my readers

The Ivy Morgan is a series about magic and witches but it's also a series about finding yourself and learning how to love. Therefore, Ivy's magical abilities are something that will grow as her relationship with Jack grows. She doesn't start out as a powerful witch, but each book will allow her to grow into the witch she's destined to become.

What does that mean?

Magic is present in the first book, but it's not the main focus. Ivy and Jack are. In future installments the magic will grow along with the way they feel about each other. You'll be able to see dream walking, ghostly possession, and second sight as Ivy becomes more comfortable in her own skin.

It's not all going to happen in one book, though.

Each book is its own contained mystery. The overall romantic arc grows with each book. If you want a lot of magic right from the start you're probably not going to like this series, and I apologize.

I hope you enjoy my new world.

Thank you for reading.

Lily Harper Hart

One

"Welcome to Shadow Lake."

Jack Harker glanced around, unsure what his new partner, Brian Nixon, was getting at. "I've seen the town before. I came up here for an interview. It's not exactly … surprising."

For his part, Brian was both amused and blasé. Since he'd hit the age of fifty a few months before, he found entertainment in witnessing others react to certain things. Watching a younger man who spent all of his thirty years in a busy city adjust to small town life was going to be entertaining. He just knew it. "It's probably a shock for you," Brian said. "Coming from Detroit to … this … is going to take a little getting used to."

Jack raised his dark eyes to Brian's mirth-filled green ones, trying to get a feel for the boisterous man. "There was a reason I wanted out of Detroit."

"I heard," Brian said, his face softening slightly. "This is still going to be … different … from what you're used to."

"I'm used to drive-by shootings, gang violence, constant robberies and one of the highest murder rates in the country," Jack said matter-of-factly. "I applied for the detective's position here because I was tired of all of that."

Brian smirked. "Well, the good news is we rarely get a murder," he said. "That's not to say we never get a murder, mind you. Just last year Layla Crowe shot her husband because she found out he was stepping out on her with Maisie Washington."

"Did she try to hide it?"

"Oh, no," Brian said. "We didn't even know the husband was dead until Layla hightailed it to the library looking for Maisie. There was a standoff, but Layla eventually surrendered."

"Was Maisie at the library?"

"She's the librarian."

"Oh," Jack said, furrowing his brow. "I thought librarians were supposed to be meek and staid."

"Not Maisie," Brian said. "She's a little ... different."

"I can't wait to meet her."

"I'm sure she'll be stopping by your place with a casserole any day now," Brian said. "She likes to ... welcome ... the new men in town before they get a chance to hear about her reputation. You're going to be right up her alley."

"I'm not sure what that means."

"In case you haven't noticed, there aren't a lot of single men in Shadow Lake," Brian said. "This is a place where people move to raise a family, not go searching for someone to build one with."

"That's why I'm here," Jack said, letting his gaze bounce around the quaint downtown. "That's exactly why I'm here."

Brian knew the real reason Jack left the Detroit Police Department a few months before, a horrific betrayal and bullet wound forcing him into early retirement. Since he barely knew the man, though, he wasn't ready to press him on the issue. He could tell Jack was keeping his cards close to his vest right now, and he really didn't blame him. "Well, how about we do a small walking tour and I'll give you the lowdown on Shadow Lake?"

"That sounds good," Jack said, falling into step next to Brian. "How long have you been here?"

"I grew up here," Brian said. "We had a farm on the south side of town when I was a kid, and that's where I live now."

"Are your parents still alive?"

"They are," Brian said. "They moved to a smaller house, though. It's a few miles away from the farm, and they come out whenever they want. This is northern Lower Michigan, though, so the winters are brutal. Once November hits, they're pretty much Florida bound until May."

"Do you like that?"

"I like knowing that my father isn't out trying to shovel snow in his seventies," Brian said. "That does not stop him from coming out and doing work in the fields during the summer, though. You can take the farmer out of Michigan for the winters, but you can't taking the farming out of a Michigan man in the summers – especially if he really loves the farm."

"So … you're a detective with the Shadow Lake Police Department and you're a farmer?" Jack looked impressed.

"I don't do a lot of the farming these days," Brian said. "I have sons, and we don't have near the crops we used to. My wife likes to do vegetables, and we have a little bit of livestock. It's not the same work my dad used to do on a daily basis."

"Still … that sounds nice."

"I heard you bought the old Winstead house on the lake," Brian said. "That's a beautiful setting, but last time I was around those parts that house needed some work. Has it been fixed up at all?"

"I'm doing that myself," Jack said. "I like to keep my hands busy."

"And you know how to renovate a house?"

Jack snickered. "Do you think because I'm a city boy that I don't know how to use a hammer?"

"Maybe," Brian conceded.

"I know how to use a hammer," Jack said. "My father owns a construction business down in St. Clair Shores."

"And that's close to the city?"

Jack rolled his eyes. "Do all country folk think the suburbs and Detroit are the same thing?"

Brian shrugged. "I am a cliché."

"The suburbs are nice," Jack said, not taking Brian's comment personally. "My parents live on Lake St. Clair, and there's a lot of new construction going on in the northern suburbs. I worked for him as a teenager – and when I had breaks from college – so I know a little bit about construction."

"Still, that house needs a lot of work."

"I'm looking forward to it," Jack said. "I figure it will keep me busy."

Brian studied his new partner for a moment, not missing the haunted look that momentarily flitted across the man's face. "I'm sure it will," he said. "If you need supplies, my brother is a manager at the Home Depot over in Traverse City. He can get you whatever you need for cost."

Jack seemed surprised by the offer. "Really?"

"That's what partners are for," Brian said. "Also, you're going to want to make yourself available for a dinner in the next week or so. My wife Millie is dying to meet you, and she's insistent on feeding people when she meets them."

Jack wanted to argue, his mouth already open with an excuse to get out of dinner, but he backed down immediately. He'd moved to Shadow Lake because he was trying to put his rampant suspicion regarding others behind him. This seemed like a good place to start. "That sounds nice."

Brian grinned. "Good. You'll like Millie. She's a good woman, and she's an amazing cook. Why do you think I need to have my pants let out once a year?" Brian gestured toward his rounded midriff.

"Just give me a few days to get settled," Jack said. "Everything I own is still in boxes."

"Sure," Brian said. "Now … on with the tour. As you can see here, this is City Hall. It also doubles as the police department."

"I've noticed," Jack replied dryly.

"Over there you have Sam's Diner. It's … well … diner food. It's all good, though, and it's a happening coffee place in the morning. If you're ever looking for someone to question, you can usually find them in the diner between seven and ten in the morning."

"Good to know." Jack was enjoying Brian's take on the town.

"That over there is the library," Brian said, pointing. "It's actually a popular spot – mostly because we don't have any place else for people to hang out. Don't go in there if you don't want Maisie Washington to jump you behind the stacks."

"I'm starting to like the sound of this Maisie woman," Jack said. "What does she look like?"

"Oh, she's a pretty one," Brian said. "There's also a reason she's still single. She's kind of one of those women who just sucks the life out of a man and then tosses him over her shoulder like an empty beer can and moves on."

"Thanks for the warning."

"She's broken more men than professional wrestling."

This time Jack couldn't swallow his laughter. "I see you don't have a very high opinion of her."

"She's broken up a few marriages," Brian said. "She also broke up my son's engagement. She's ... not my favorite person."

"Well, I wouldn't worry about it," Jack said. "I'm not really looking to date anyone."

"Are you saying you're a bachelor for life?" Brian arched an inquisitive eyebrow.

"Probably," Jack conceded. "I just don't think I'm relationship material. I've never met a woman who can hold my interest for more than a few weeks. I don't particularly want to hurt anyone – or let anyone get attached to me – so I'm planning to keep myself out of the dating pool in Shadow Lake for the foreseeable future."

"Maybe you *are* a good match for Maisie," Brian mused.

Jack chuckled. "Even if I was open to dating – which I'm not, so don't let your wife try to set me up with anyone – I don't think Maisie sounds like my type."

"What makes you think my wife would try to set you up with someone?"

"It's just a feeling," Jack said, holding up his hand. "Don't worry. I'm not insinuating your wife is meddlesome ... despite what I've heard about country women."

"Oh, she's meddlesome," Brian said. "She's got a whole list of women she wants to pair you up with. She just wants to meet you before she decides on one."

"I think I'll pass," Jack said.

"I'll let you tell Millie that," Brian said. "She takes bad news better from strangers than she does from me."

"I'm looking forward to that conversation," Jack deadpanned.

"You'll survive," Brian said. "Okay, that's the stable. There are about ten horses in there, and if you're stuck on something to do when Millie forces you on a blind date, that's always a good idea. It's only open for about six months out of the year. The barn next to it is where they hold the town dances."

Jack jerked his head up. "Where do they keep the feed for the horses?"

"In the stable."

"Are you honestly saying that Shadow Lake has town dances?"

"Every week in the summer," Brian said. "There's not a lot of things here for the kids to do. The nearest theater is still an hour away, and the nearest mall is almost two hours away. This is the sticks, son."

"So … the kids here go to weekly dances? That's not what we did when we were teenagers."

"Oh, they do that, too," Brian said. "There's a make-out spot on the east side of town. It's on that bluff you pass when you're driving into town. Friday and Saturday nights are busy up there when the weather is nice."

Jack racked his brain but came up empty when he tried to picture the spot. "Do they get rowdy up there?"

"No," Brian said, shaking his head. "It's mostly just heavy breathing and groping. There have been a few problems with fathers when they catch their beloved daughters rolling around with the local boys, though. So that's one thing to keep in mind. Oh, and most of the fathers here are armed so … ."

"Be careful?"

"They usually don't shoot law enforcement," Brian said. "They might shoot a few rounds into the air, though. Just be prepared."

Jack nodded. "Okay. Anything else?"

"There's also a party spot on the west side of the lake," Brian said. "It's in an area the kids think is secret, and it is hard to access unless you're on foot."

"If you know where it is, why not shut them down?"

"It's just easier knowing where they are," Brian said. "Teenagers are going to party. It's what they do. Right now they're camping out there and not driving, so we kind of let things go as long as they're not being too rowdy. If things get out of hand, we'll bust them, and then they'll just find another party spot. It's spring, so they're just getting started this year."

"Okay," Jack said. "That doesn't sound too hard."

"It's not," Brian said. "Your biggest problem is probably going to be senior citizens driving when they shouldn't be and the occasional livestock versus automobile accident. There are a few domestic incidents each month, and some of the elderly women on the library committee like to throw down, but that's about it."

"The library committee?"

"It's really just an excuse to have tea with bourbon in it," Brian said. "They never do anything to help the library."

"So why keep the committee intact?"

Brian shrugged. "Why not?"

Jack couldn't come up with a viable reason so he let it go. "So basically we just patrol the town and keep everyone from fighting with each other. That's what you're saying, right?"

"Pretty much," Brian confirmed.

That sounded absolutely perfect to Jack. "I'm looking forward to it."

"We'll see if you feel the same way in a week," Brian said. "It's a beautiful town, but you have to come up with your own way to entertain yourself."

"That's just the way I like it," Jack said. "Why do you think I bought a house that needs so much work?"

"I think you fancy yourself a loner," Brian said. "I'm just not sure if you really are one yet."

"I am."

"Well … then good luck to you."

"Thanks."

After finishing their loop around town, which took a grand total of fifteen minutes – and that included stopping to talk to some downtown regulars – Jack and Brian found themselves back in front of the police department.

"Well … ." Brian didn't get a chance to finish his sentence because Ava Moffett, the department secretary, stuck her head out the door and fixed her attention on him. "What's wrong? Is Billy Calhoun out trying to romance Joe Henderson's cows again?"

Jack fought the mad urge to laugh at the visual. He had no idea who Billy Calhoun was, but he was dying to meet him now.

"No," Ava said, shaking her head. "Ivy Morgan called."

Brian lifted his head, surprised. "Ivy? What's wrong with her? She never gets in any trouble."

"Well, that's a matter of opinion," Ava said. "You know my feelings on that subject."

"I do," Brian said. "I think you're being a pill where Ivy is concerned. What's up?"

"She says there's a body at the end of her driveway," Ava said.

"A body?"

"As in a dead person," Ava said. "If you ask me, she probably did it."

"We didn't ask you, Ava," Brian said. "Call her back and tell her we're on our way."

"You know she's a minion of Hell, right?" Ava wasn't backing down.

"Thank you, Ava," Brian said, testy. "We'll take it from here."

Ava's face was hard to read as she turned on her heel and stalked back inside the building. When she was gone, Jack turned his studied gaze to Brian. "What was all that about?"

"There's one other thing I should probably tell you about Shadow Lake," Brian said.

Jack waited.

"Let's do it in the car," Brian said. "It's a short ride and a not-so-long story."

"Just give me a hint."

"Well … Ivy Morgan is a witch."

That was the one thing Jack wasn't expecting. It seemed Shadow Lake wasn't going to be quite as boring as he initially envisioned.

Two

"Are you going to tell me about the witch?"

After climbing into Brian's patrol car and watching him navigate the country roads for five minutes, Jack was at his wit's end. He was dying to know what Brian meant when he called Ivy a "witch."

"She's a witch," Brian said, shrugging. "She's one of those nature-loving tree huggers who walks around in ankle-length skirts and pets trees because she doesn't want people to cut them down. She's kind of a … hippie."

"You said she was a witch, though," Jack pointed out.

"I think the politically correct term is Wiccan," Brian said. "I don't think she's really a witch. I haven't heard of any broom flying going on."

"Ava seems to think differently."

"That's because Ava and Ivy went to high school together and all the boys in school had a thing for Ivy," Brian said. "Ava was convinced it was because Ivy was casting spells on them. She refuses to believe it was simply because Ivy was low maintenance and … well … quite the looker."

Jack was intrigued, despite himself. "Go on."

"Well, you see, Ivy was always a free-spirited kid," Brian said. "She refused to do the stuff the other kids were doing. Sometimes I think it was out of spite. While all the fifth graders spent the summer at church camp, Ivy spent her summer creating a fairy ring in the woods next to her house."

"A fairy ring?"

"It's some … garden thing," Brian said. "It's actually pretty beautiful. I saw it once. She still keeps it up. I think she goes out there to read in the summer."

"I don't understand how that makes her a witch," Jack said.

"It doesn't," Brian said. "People just think she's a witch because she identifies herself as Wiccan and she looks like a hippie. Well, and she doesn't go to church."

Jack arched an eyebrow. "That makes her a witch?"

"This is a Christian town," Brian replied. "You can be a Baptist, Catholic, Methodist, or Missionary … we even have a group of Jehovah's Witnesses who live on the outskirts of town … but you have to be a Christian."

"That sounds a little *rigid* to me," Jack said. "It doesn't sound like this woman is doing anything wrong."

"She never does anything wrong," Brian said. "She's loud … and opinionated … and don't you dare ever litter in front of her because she doesn't like it, but she's a good woman."

"How well do you know her?"

"I know her parents," Brian said. "We're about the same age, and we went to school together. Michael and Luna have always been … free-spirited."

"Is that code for something?"

"They're hippies, and they raised their kids to be hippies," Brian said. "Ivy does whatever she wants to do, and she says whatever comes to her mind. She's ruffled the occasional feather because she doesn't tow the town line."

"I'm still waiting for the bad part," Jack said.

"Despite her … peculiarities … Ivy is still pretty popular," Brian said. "It might be because she runs the best nursery in the entire state and she can make anything grow."

"Why else?"

"Every single man in her age group has tried to date her – including my sons," Brian said. "There's just something about her. I don't know how to explain it."

"Do you want to be more specific?"

"You'll see for yourself," Brian said. "I wouldn't be surprised if one look at her changes your mind about dating in Shadow Lake."

Jack snorted. "I can pretty much guarantee that's not going to be the case," he said. "I have nothing against dating a witch. I wasn't joking about wanting to stay away from romantic stuff in general, though."

"We'll see," Brian said.

IVY MORGAN PACED THE END OF HER DRIVEWAY AS SHE waited for the arrival of local law enforcement. Given the size of Shadow Lake, she was having trouble understanding how it could take anyone more than five minutes to get to her house.

Her ankle-length gypsy skirt rustled around her ankles as she moved, and her bare feet padded silently on the gravel. Ivy was so worked up she didn't even register the pain as the rocks pressed into the soft soles of her feet.

Back and forth. Back and forth.

Where are they?

When Brian's cruiser finally crested the hill, Ivy let loose with a heavy sigh. She watched as Brian parked the car, her gaze landing on the man in the passenger seat as she tried to hold on to her righteous indignation. It was hard because the handsome stranger was … breathtaking. Ivy could practically feel the masculinity rolling off of him.

He was dressed down in simple blue jeans and a button-down shirt. His brown hair was a little long, shaggy even. His brown eyes were the color of molten chocolate, though, and his chest was broad and strong.

The second Ivy's blue eyes met his it was as if she could practically feel the magic zipping between them. There was a connection there she couldn't put a name to. She had a feeling it was purely sexual, though, and that thought threw her. She was not in the mood for … this.

Instead of focusing on that, though, Ivy decided to do the only thing she could do: complain. "Well … it took you long enough."

Brian graced Ivy with a small smile, taking in her bare feet and long dark hair – which was highlighted with bright pink streaks that caused the little old ladies in town to frown whenever they saw her – as she placed her hands on her hips and regarded him with irrepressible anger. "How are you, Ivy?"

"I called ten minutes ago and said I found a body," Ivy replied, darting occasional looks at Jack out of the corner of her eye. *Who is he?* "I don't understand what took you so long."

"I was giving my new partner here a tour of the town," Brian said. "Jack Harker, meet Ivy Morgan."

Jack regarded Ivy with unreadable eyes. "Ma'am."

Ivy made a face. "Ma'am? How old do I look to you?"

"It's just a term of respect, ma'am," Jack said. "There was no offense meant."

Who is this guy? Ivy brushed her hair away from her face, giving in to an urge to look Jack up and down one more time before turning back to Brian. "A tour of the town takes two minutes."

"I can see you're worked up, Ivy," Brian said. "Why don't you show us what you found that you think is a body?"

"I'm sorry, *think*? Are you insinuating that I'm making up finding a body?"

Brian held up his hands in mock surrender. "No, of course not. I just can't remember the last time someone stumbled over a dead body at the end of their driveway." Brian glanced around pointedly. "I'm still not seeing a body."

Ivy narrowed her eyes, irked. "I'm going to expect your apology in exactly five seconds," she said, stalking to the opposite side of the driveway and pointing toward the narrow ditch on the other side.

Brian moved to the spot Ivy indicated, lowering his gaze to the ground. Jack joined him, and they both sucked in a breath when their eyes fell on the battered body of a woman. She was fully clothed – which was a good thing – but her body was partially covered by branches and debris, which would seem to indicate someone had tried to hide it. Since decomposition wasn't pronounced, the body couldn't have been there for long, but there were some angry purple bruises poking out through the debris – and matted blood on the visible sections of clothing. That meant someone had either dumped the woman out here and tried to cover it up or killed her in this location and tried to do the same. Either way, it wasn't good.

"Well?" Ivy crossed her arms over her chest and tapped her foot.

"I stand corrected," Brian said, kneeling down. "I'm sorry. This is definitely a body."

JACK WAS HAVING A HARD TIME TEARING HIS ATTENTION AWAY from Ivy long enough to focus on the body. Even though he'd seen more than his fair share of death during his tenure in Detroit, the sight always jolted him. The fact that this one showed up in one of the most serene locations he'd ever seen was troubling.

Jack looked Ivy up and down, taking in her Bohemian appearance with a studied eye. Brian wasn't lying when he said she was beautiful. The woman standing next to him was nothing short of striking. Her long hair was streaked with pink, and while he'd always thought that looked tacky on many, she somehow made it work. Her purple skirt was long and billowy, and every time the wind blew it up slightly, Jack caught a glimpse of a pair of shapely legs beneath.

Ivy was wearing a basic black tank top, but her lithe frame was strong and well defined. She obviously kept herself in shape and, despite himself, Jack couldn't help but be a little interested. He had no idea why. The last thing he wanted was a romantic entanglement.

Maybe she is a witch, he internally mused.

"We need to call the county crime scene techs out here," Brian said. "We need photos and measurements taken before we can move the body." He turned to Ivy. "Did you touch her?"

Ivy pressed her lips together and didn't immediately answer.

"Ivy?" Brian pressed.

"I checked to make sure she was really dead," Ivy said, exhaling heavily. "I … I've never seen a dead body before. She looked dead, but I had to be sure."

Brian nodded. "Okay. Where did you touch her?"

Ivy pointed. "Just on her wrist."

"Okay," Brian said. "Do you know who it is?"

Ivy shook her head. "I don't think so. I couldn't … look at her for too long, though."

"When was the last time you were down here?" Jack asked, finally opening his mouth after what seemed like forever. His deep baritone was enough to draw Ivy's attention back to him.

"I come down here every day to check the mailbox," Ivy said. "Well … I guess I don't on Sundays. I was down here yesterday, though, and she wasn't here then."

"I'm not an expert," Brian said, straightening. "I don't think she's been dead for twenty-four hours, though."

"No," Jack agreed. "I'm guessing she's only been out here for six to eight hours."

"Do you think she was killed here?" Ivy asked, worrying her bottom lip with her teeth.

"I don't know," Jack replied. "We need to figure out how she died first. She's pretty covered up here, and I don't want to risk moving any of those branches or leaves until the coroner gets here. We don't want to disturb the evidence."

Ivy nodded. That made sense. Still … . "If she was killed here, shouldn't I have been able to hear her screaming or something from my house?" She cast a worried gaze at her cottage. "I wasn't that far away."

Brian patted Ivy's shoulder sympathetically. "Ivy, I know you think it's your job to help everyone who needs it, but odds are that you would have been hurt, too if you tried to intervene."

"That doesn't make me feel better," Ivy said.

"I know it doesn't," Brian said. "It's still the way of the world. What I need you to do now is go inside and put some shoes on. You shouldn't be traipsing around out here with bare feet."

"I'm fine." Ivy waved off his concern.

"I'm sure you are," Brian said, tugging on his patience. "You might be stepping on evidence, though. There also might be some sort of weapon out here. Just because we haven't seen anything … ."

"That doesn't mean it's not out here," Jack finished.

Ivy balked. "I'm sorry. I didn't think about that. I'll go back to the cottage now."

"Jack will go with you," Brian said.

Jack swiveled, fixing Brian with a curious look. "I will?"

"She needs to be questioned," Brian said, unruffled. "You can do that while I wait for the coroner and crime scene team. The locals are going to start showing up in droves when word of this gets out. We need to try and be as quick as we can."

Understanding washed over Jack. "It's a small town," he said. "They're not going to have anything better to do."

"This is the biggest thing to hit Shadow Lake in years," Brian said. "They're not going to be able to stop themselves from coming out and gawking."

"Of course," Jack said. He swept his arm out to usher Ivy forward. "After you, ma'am."

Ivy scowled. "If you keep calling me that we're going to have a problem."

Jack swallowed his smile. Brian was right. There was *something* about her. It was just something he couldn't entertain. Still … she was definitely nice to look at.

Three

"This is a nice place," Jack said, glancing around Ivy's quaint cottage with unveiled interested. "It's actually … beautiful."

"Thank you," Ivy said, shuffling toward the kitchen. "My Dad refinished the entire house when we were kids. This is all his work, although I decorated it."

"Are your parents … gone?"

"They don't live here, if that's what you're asking," Ivy said. "They're not gone, though. They're still in town. They just moved to a different house and sold me this one so I could be close to the nursery."

"It's really nice," Jack said, running his hands over the ornate wood molding that separated the living room and kitchen. "I love the setting of the cottage. I like how it's close to the road, but you can't really see it. It's like you're living in the middle of the woods … but you're not."

"That's why I love it, too," Ivy said, arching an eyebrow as she watched him. "Where are you from?"

Jack jerked his attention away from the doorframe and fixed it on Ivy. "What makes you think I'm not from around here?"

"I can spot a city boy from a mile away," Ivy said, smiling. The expression lit up her whole face, and for a second Jack lost himself in her exuberant grin.

He shook himself out of his reverie. "I grew up in a suburb of Detroit," Jack said. "I was with the Detroit police department until …"

Ivy narrowed her eyes, sensing he was about to say something he would regret. He caught himself, though.

"I just wanted an easier life," Jack said. "I've always loved this part of the state. I saw the ad for the detective's position in the newspaper and I applied and … well … here I am."

"I guess that's our gain," Ivy said, moving into the kitchen. "Do you want something to drink?"

"I'm fine."

"I have iced tea, green tea, peach tea, and tomato juice."

Jack made a face. "Tomato juice?"

"It's my favorite juice," Ivy said, opening the refrigerator door. "Do you want something to drink or not?"

"I'm fine."

Ivy ignored him and poured two glasses of iced tea. Once she turned her back to return the glass jug to the refrigerator, a black cat jumped up onto the counter and fixed his attention on the tea. When Ivy turned back around she already had her finger extended in the cat's direction. "Don't you even think about it, Nicodemus."

The cat arched his back, an innocent look on his face as he tried to get Ivy to pet him. Ivy gave in and rubbed him twice. "You're not supposed to be on the counter."

Nicodemus cried plaintively.

"I'll feed you in a little bit," Ivy said. "For now, you need to get off the counter."

Jack fought the urge to roll his eyes as he watched Ivy interact with the animal. He'd never met a cat that did what it was told. It just wasn't in their nature. That's why, as Ivy moved toward him with the drinks in her hands, he had to tamp down his disbelief as the cat jumped down from the counter and disappeared down a short hallway that Jack assumed led to Ivy's bedroom. "How did you do that?"

"Do what?" Ivy asked, her face blank.

"You told the cat to get down from the counter and he did it."

"I asked nicely," Ivy replied, nonplussed. "When you ask nicely, you'd be surprised how things turn out."

Jack took the proffered glass of iced tea with a small nod of thank you, but he never moved his eyes from Ivy's face. "You're … interesting."

"So I've been told," Ivy said, smiling tightly. "I'm sure you've already heard that I'm a witch."

"I might have heard something," Jack admitted, sitting in one of the chairs around the kitchen table as Ivy settled next to him. "Ava mentioned something when she came to find us about your call."

"Ava," Ivy said, nodding sagely. "That doesn't surprise me. We've never had the … warmest … of relationships."

"Brian filled me in on some of that while we were driving out here," Jack said. "I'm sorry things have been so difficult for you."

Ivy made a face. "I'm happy with who I am," she said. "Things were never difficult for me because I wouldn't let them be. I'm happy with my life and beliefs. If other people don't like it … well … that's their problem."

Jack liked her attitude, even if he wasn't sure she was being entirely truthful. You could be completely happy with yourself and still hurt by the words and actions of others. "You stand out in an area like this," he said. "Have you ever considered moving south? You would fit right in down there. The city would love you."

"I love the country," Ivy replied, blasé. "The country loves me, too. There are some people that don't understand me. I really don't worry about them, though."

Jack nodded thoughtfully. He was having trouble tearing his gaze from the high ridges of her cheeks, or the oceans of blue beckoning to him in her eyes.

"Did you have questions you wanted to ask?" Ivy asked, breaking the silence.

"Um … yeah," Jack replied, returning to the moment. "Can you tell me what you were doing last night?"

"I finished up at the greenhouse around six," Ivy said. "I had a quick dinner and then I went for a walk in the woods. I got back home around ten or so, and then I read a book on my back patio. I was in bed by midnight."

"You went for a walk in the woods alone? After dark?" Jack couldn't help but be dubious. In the city, it was never wise to walk alone – no matter what neighborhood you were in. People didn't always live by that rule, but it was a smart one to follow.

"I grew up in this house," Ivy said. "I know these woods like the back of my hand. I like to walk. It's how I keep in shape. I don't really think about it now."

"Okay," Jack said, readjusting his thinking. "Did you hear anything last night?"

"No," Ivy said, shaking her head and causing her long hair to brush against her shoulders. "I sleep like the dead, though. I sleep with a fan. I like the white noise. Between that and Nicodemus purring, I really never wake up."

"And … um … were you alone?" Jack told himself he was asking the question out of professional necessity, but he honestly wasn't so sure.

"I was alone," Ivy confirmed.

"You're not dating anyone? I'm only asking because I want to be able to ascertain if someone has the ability to come and go from the property without piquing your interest."

Ivy pressed her lips together, and for a second Jack wondered if she believed him. When she opened her mouth again to speak, he couldn't hide his relief.

"There's no one spending the night here," Ivy said. "It's just me."

Jack nodded. "Okay. Well … I'm sure we'll be in touch. For the time being, I think it would be wise to keep your nocturnal walks to a minimum. There could be someone dangerous out in these woods."

"I'll take it under advisement."

Jack stilled. "I'm not trying to tell you what to do. I just … ."

"You don't know me," Ivy said. "It's okay. This is my home, though. If you don't feel safe in your home there's no sense in living there. Nothing will stop me from walking through the woods."

"But … ."

Ivy held up her hand. "If it will make you feel better, I promise to be careful."

Jack wasn't sure that did make him feel better. Something told him it was the best he was going to get, though.

"WHEN WILL THEY DO THE AUTOPSY?" JACK ASKED, SLIDING into his new desk chair and rocking back and forth to see if it was comfortable.

"Probably not until tomorrow," Brian said, dropping a file on his desk and glancing around. "It's not like down south. We have limited resources."

"Sorry I was inside so long," Jack said. "I just had a few questions to ask Ms. Morgan."

"I'm sure," Brian said, pursing his lips.

"What is that supposed to mean?" Jack leaned forward, agitated.

"It doesn't mean anything," Brian said, holding up his hand. "I just thought I might have sensed a little something between you and Ivy."

"A little something?"

"Chemistry," Brian replied, guileless.

"We talked for five minutes in front of you and you think you saw chemistry? Are you sure your wife is the only meddlesome one?" Jack was going for levity, but he didn't miss the uptick of his heartbeat.

"Listen, I'm not telling you how to live your life," Brian said. "It's none of my business if you want to go to bed alone every night for the rest of your life. That doesn't change the fact that I saw you looking at Ivy. Don't feel bad about it. She's a beautiful woman."

"She's ... okay," Jack said carefully.

Brian snorted. "Yeah. She's ... okay."

Jack rolled his eyes. "She's still just a woman," he said. "I'm not interested in a relationship. I already told you that. I have my reasons."

Brian's face softened. If any man had reasons to build a wall around his heart it was Jack Harker. Still, he'd definitely witnessed something today – and it wasn't just on Jack's part. "Well, if you're not interested in Ivy, you might want to find a way to let her down easy," he said, changing tactics.

Jack stilled. "Excuse me?"

"You weren't the only one I was feeling chemistry from," Brian said. "Ivy couldn't take her eyes off you either. You should be proud. I can't remember the last time someone turned that girl's head."

Jack's chest puffed out, if only in his mind. *Was that true?* "I don't think she was any more interested in me than I was in her. She's a nice woman. She has a certain … flair. I'm still not interested."

"Of course you're not," Brian said. "You're set in your ways. There's no way a woman could change that."

"There's not," Jack said. "I can't even think about something like that right now. I just … ."

Brian's face fell, instantly contrite. "I'm sorry. I guess I never considered why you wouldn't want to deal with something like that right now. Still, being alone isn't the way to a happy life."

"What makes you think I want a happy life?"

"Everyone does."

"I don't think that's in the cards for me," Jack said honestly. "I don't have any grand dreams for a happy ending … or a white picket fence … or a wife and kids. I just want a little … peace."

Brian's heart rolled. He'd never known someone to give up on dreaming. The idea made him sad. "You might change your mind," he said. "If you do, I'm just saying that Ivy Morgan might be a nice place to start dreaming again."

"Because she's a witch?" Jack's eyes were twinkling.

"Because she's a good woman," Brian said. "And, much like you, she doesn't care about fitting in."

"Who says I don't care?"

"Your face," Brian said, snickering. "Just get settled and think about it. I would hate to think of you going through life alone. I don't want to think of Ivy doing it either, and I wasn't lying about her turning up her nose at almost every man who has ever tried to go after her."

"I'm sure Ivy doesn't want to put up with my problems any more than I want to deal with her … specific brand of oddness."

"Whatever," Brian said. "I … ." He snapped his mouth shut when

Ava sashayed into the room with a manila folder in her hand. "What's up?"

Ava's face contorted. "Aren't you ever happy to see me? Not even once?"

"Not generally," Brian said. "You're usually up to no good."

"That's just a horrible thing to say," Ava said. "I don't appreciate you talking badly about me."

"You'll live," Brian said, extending his hand. "What is that?"

"It's some file the coroner's assistant dropped off," Ava said, wrinkling her nose. "He seemed to think you'd want to see it right away."

Brian took the file and opened it, his eyes widening as he scanned the photographs inside. "Well, holy ... ."

Jack leaned over, interested. "What is it?"

Ava smiled at him, the expression bright and flirtatious. It seemed Ivy wasn't the only one to take a shine to Shadow Lake's newest resident, Brian mused. He couldn't focus on that now, though. Brian handed the photos over to his new partner, and as soon as Jack focused on them he leaned forward.

"What are these?"

"They look like evil symbols," Ava replied.

Brian glared at her. "Did you look in that file?"

"The photos just slipped out," Ava said.

"You're not supposed to look in a private file," Brian snapped. "That's not part of your job description."

"Take it up with the chief."

Brian scowled. That was a sticky situation, especially since the chief also happened to be Ava's father. That was how she got the job in the first place. "I will." Dan Moffett may be Ava's father, but he was also Brian's longtime friend. "He and I will definitely be having a talk."

Ava shot him a look. "Don't you threaten me."

Brian ignored her and turned his attention back to Jack. "What do you think?"

"I think these symbols look ... satanic."

"That's what I thought when I saw them," Brian agreed.

"Well, that makes sense," Ava said. "They were found carved into the skin of a woman whose body just happened to be found on Ivy Morgan's property. She's your suspect."

"Do you really think Ivy is capable of killing someone?" Brian asked.

"Of course," Ava said. "She's a Devil worshipper. That's what they do. Mark my words: Ivy Morgan is not only responsible for this dead girl, but she'll be responsible for the next one, too. She's evil … and she's just getting started."

Four

"Hey there, pop tart."

Ivy lowered the book she was reading and glared at her older brother with unveiled disgust. "I hate it when you call me that, Max."

"I know," Max said, tousling Ivy's hair with one hand while he clasped a brown paper bag in the other. "I brought dinner."

Ivy wrinkled her nose, torn. She wasn't in the mood to deal with her brother – or the drama he often brought into her life – but she also wasn't particularly looking forward to cooking for herself. It was a hard choice. "What did you bring me?"

"A Greek salad and tomato soup from the diner."

Well, that did it. There was no way she could turn down her favorite soup. "Sold," Ivy said, leaning forward so she could reach for the bag. When Max jerked it away from her, she scowled. "What are you doing? I thought you were here to feed me."

"I am here to feed you," Max said, studying Ivy's face soberly. "I'm also here to see if you're okay. I can't feed you until I'm sure you're all right."

"What makes you think I'm not okay?" Ivy asked, averting her blue eyes from the matching set her brother sported.

"You found a dead body today," Max said. "You were the talk of the town."

"Aren't I always?"

"Only when I'm not vying for top billing," Max said, tilting his dark head to the side. "How are you really feeling?"

"Conflicted," Ivy admitted, dropping the book on the small table next to her lounge chair. "I can't help but wonder if she was killed in my front yard."

"And if she was, you want to know if there's something you could've done to save her," Max said. "I get it, Ivy. The thing is, I'm glad you didn't hear anything."

"But I could have saved her."

"You don't know that, Ivy," Max said. "You might want to believe otherwise, but there's no way of knowing that. Personally, I think you might have ended up in the ditch right next to her. As much trouble as you are – and you are a big, old barrel of it – I still couldn't imagine my life without you."

"I thought you told Mom and Dad that you wanted to give me back to Santa Claus one Christmas. Didn't you want to exchange me for a truck?"

"It was a whole package of Matchbox cars, actually. Get it right," Max said, smirking. "There's no accounting for taste. If you must know, I would have regretted that trade after a few years."

"Years?"

"Matchbox cars are built to last, pop tart."

Ivy rolled her eyes. "You're unbelievable."

"I try." Max tugged on a strand of Ivy's hair. "I do love you, Ivy."

"I love you, too."

"Good," Max said. "Now I'm going to feed you."

"How did you know I hadn't eaten yet?"

"Because I know the way your mind works," Max said, digging into the bag and doling out the food. "You would have just gnawed on this until you couldn't take it for another second. Then you'd have gone for a hike in the woods. Then you would have gone to bed hungry. I know you better than you know yourself sometimes."

"You don't know everything."

"I know enough," Max countered. "So, you're going to eat your dinner, and then we're going to go for your nightly walk together."

"I'm perfectly capable of walking alone," Ivy said, irritation building. "I don't need a babysitter."

"Don't think of it as babysitting," Max said, winking. "Think of it as me being bigger than you and you not having a choice."

Ivy crossed her arms over her chest. "That's worse."

"I know," Max said. "That's why I want you to think about it that way."

"We should've exchanged you for those Matchbox cars when I was a kid."

"It's too late now."

"THAT was good," Ivy admitted, finishing the final bite of salad and resting her fork against the table. "I didn't realize how hungry I was."

"That's because you're more interested in taking care of others than yourself," Max said, wiping the grease from his hamburger from his chin. "Why do you think you have me?"

"I thought it was so my ego never got out of hand," Ivy teased.

"Even I'm not up for that task," Max said. "Tell me about the new cop."

Ivy faltered, her chest inexplicably warming at the thought of Jack Harker. She had no idea why, but the mere mention of the man was enough to give her heart a little flutter. "What do you mean?"

Max's face was unreadable. "I heard he was out here with Brian Nixon," he replied, oblivious. "I want to know what he's like. I hear there's already a rush to get the first date with him. I think Maisie and Ava are working the hardest, but I heard all the women at the hair salon are planning to take him dinners this week."

Ivy made a face. "He seemed … fine."

"I need more than that," Max said. "Is he competition for me?"

"Competition?" Ivy was confused.

"I'm the most eligible bachelor in town," Max said. "I like my title. I've heard this guy could give me a run for my money. I wouldn't mind foisting Maisie and Ava off on him, but I like the rest of my harem as it is."

Sometimes Ivy didn't understand men, and this was one of those times. She couldn't hide her scowl as she tried to tamp down her irritation. "Harem? Do you have any idea how insulting that is?"

"I think it just bothers you because you're a feminist."

"I'm not a feminist ... well, I am ... but you're still a pig," Ivy shot back. "That's just really insulting."

"Is he better looking than me or not?" Max asked, nonplussed. "That's all I want to know."

"I don't think I'm the best judge of that," Ivy said, skirting around the question.

"Why?"

"Because you're my brother," Ivy replied. "I'm incapable of being attracted to you. It's not a level playing field."

"Oh, crap," Max grumbled. "I heard he was good looking. This is going to tick me off. It's going to totally ruin my summer. I can just feel it. I'm going to have to go back to the gym and bulk up."

Ivy grinned, love for her brother and his outrageous outlook on life bubbling up. "I'm sure you'll be okay," she said. "The women are always going to love you. They can't help it. You're just ... lovable."

"I am lovable," Max agreed, leaning back in his chair and letting his gaze shift to the woods. The sun was setting, and the fading light cast an eerie pall over the trees. Max was just about to suggest starting their walk when the rest of Ivy's words washed over him. "Wait a second. You said you couldn't be attracted to me so it wasn't an apt comparison. Does that mean you're attracted to him?"

Ivy jumped to her feet and started collecting the empty food containers. "Are you ready for our walk?"

JACK PARKED ON THE STREET IN FRONT OF IVY'S HOUSE, BEING careful to hide his pickup truck behind a thick outcropping of trees as he studied the small cottage. He had no idea why he was out here. He kept telling himself it was out of professional curiosity, a need to see the spot where the body was found again fueling him, but he couldn't be sure that was really true.

He just had to see Ivy again. He couldn't explain it.

Jack had just about made up his mind to man up and knock on the door, thoughts of asking her to identify the symbols washing through his head as an excuse for his appearance, when he saw it open to allow Ivy's exit. Jack couldn't help but smile when he saw her, the cute skirt from earlier replaced by a pair of tight yoga pants and a T-shirt. The smile faded when he saw the man walk out of the cottage behind her. He was tall, and the way they were animatedly talking to one another left no room for confusion. Whoever he was, Ivy obviously adored him.

She'd lied to him. She *was* dating someone.

"I'M NOT TALKING ABOUT THIS WITH YOU," IVY SAID, JUMPING up on a stump so she could evade Max's sneaky hand as he reached for her. It was a brother's prerogative to put his sister in a headlock whenever the mood struck. That's what Max had told her – on a regular basis, mind you – since they were children anyway. She knew exactly what he would try to do to get her to talk.

"Don't you even try to be cute," Max said, extending his finger and wagging it in Ivy's face as she giggled. "Tell me about the cop. I want to know what you see in him."

"I didn't say I saw anything in him," Ivy argued. "You made that up in your own head."

"No, I didn't," Max said. "I know you as well as you know yourself. You have the hots for the new cop. Don't you dare lie."

"I don't have the hots for him."

"Ivy," Max warned.

"I find him … interesting."

"Define interesting."

"I can't define it," Ivy said, shifting so she could balance on one foot and stretch at the same time. She was incredibly limber, and she liked to play balancing games whenever she could. She knew it especially annoyed Max because he wasn't known for being graceful. He was a bear on the football field. Unfortunately, he was also one on the dance floor.

Max stilled, rubbing his hand against his chin as he thoughtfully studied his sister. "You haven't liked a guy in … crap … I can't remember the last guy you liked. This one must be something special."

"I barely know him," Ivy said. "I talked to him for all of ten minutes. I gave him a glass of iced tea, we talked about Nicodemus, he asked me a few questions, and then he left."

"You still like him," Max said, grinning. "Admit it."

"I don't know him," Ivy said. "I can't like him if I don't know him."

"Okay," Max said, raising his hands in mock surrender. "How about we take the word 'like' off the table. You're attracted to him. At least admit that."

"He's a handsome man," Ivy said, giving in marginally. "There's something appealing about his face."

"You can admit you think he's hot," Max said. "You don't always have to be so prim and proper."

"Fine," Ivy said, rolling her eyes. "He's hot. He's got this strong, square jaw. His hair is a little long and it's dark. His eyes are really expressive. Oh, and his body looks like he works out even more than you do."

Max scowled. "That's great."

Ivy giggled. "He also seems a little … closed off," she said. "I don't think he's looking for anyone. I think you're going to be able to keep your harem all to yourself this summer."

"Are you disappointed he's not looking for someone?"

"Of course not," Ivy scoffed. "I'm not looking for someone. I don't care if he is hot. I'm not really in the mood to … date."

"I think you're making that up," Max said. "I think you do want to date someone, but you're so used to people treating you … differently … that you've trained yourself to expect the worst when it comes to men. You don't know this guy is going to be like the other losers you've dated. It might not hurt to give him a chance."

"I don't want to give him a chance, Max," Ivy said. "I don't need a man to complete me. I'm happy with who I am."

"Fine," Max said, rolling his eyes. "I totally believe you. You're not attracted to the new cop. You don't need a man. You're perfectly happy with who you are."

"Thank you," Ivy said, jumping from the stump and hitting the ground solidly. "It's about time you actually listened to the words coming out of my mouth instead of the ones you think you hear."

"I'm ashamed of my actions," Max said.

"Let's go for our walk."

Max followed her silently. Once he was sure she was lost in her own head he grabbed her around the waist and lifted her up, twirling her around so she had no way to fight against his impressive muscle mass. "Now tell me how you really feel," he said. "Tell me how hot you think he is."

"I'm going to kill you," Ivy shrieked, but she couldn't stop herself from laughing. Max was like a dog with a bone sometimes, and this was one bone he had no intention of relinquishing – at least not any time soon.

JACK'S HEART ROLLED PAINFULLY AS HE WATCHED IVY AND HER boyfriend cavort. While she'd graced him with a few soft smiles earlier in the day, she'd never let her face brighten that way when he was around. Of course, since they were talking about a dead body at the time, that wasn't particularly surprising.

Still … seeing her with another man was enough to quell the irrational thoughts he'd been harboring for hours. She was involved. She was clearly happy. That made things so much easier in his mind.

The small voice in the back of Jack's head wouldn't stop knocking on the mental door he didn't want to open. If things were easier because she was involved, why did he feel so disappointed?

Five

"What are you doing?" Brian asked the next morning, surprised to find Jack already at his desk before he even got himself a mug of coffee.

"It's called work," Jack said, not glancing up from his computer screen. "You should try it some time."

Brian rolled his eyes. "I'm guessing you're not much of a morning person," he said. "That has to be the reason you're taking your grumpy mood out on me. That's it, right?"

Jack sucked in a breath, steadying himself. "I'm sorry. You're right. That was uncalled for. I'm just … concentrating."

"I can see that," Brian said, shuffling behind Jack's desk. "What are you concentrating on?"

"I'm trying to find a match for these symbols." Jack gestured at the photographs of the dead girl. "I'm not having a lot of luck. Have we been able to identify her yet?"

Brian shook his head. "She's not a local girl. That's all I can say with any certainty. We scanned her fingerprints and entered them into the system. We're looking for a match. If she doesn't have a record, though, we're going to have to find another way to identify her."

"And there are no missing girls who match her description in this part of the state?"

"None."

"Well ... that sucks," Jack grumbled. "It's going to be pretty darned hard to track down a motive and an assailant if we don't know who the victim is."

"I agree," Brian said. "How long have you been working on those symbols?"

"About two hours."

Brian made a face. "Don't you sleep?" He glanced at the clock on the wall. "That means you got in here at five."

Jack shrugged. "So?"

"That's five in the morning," Brian said. "You shouldn't be up at that hour, let alone at work."

"I thought you were a farmer. Aren't farmers supposed to be up at the crack of dawn? Aren't they supposed to like it?"

Brian rolled his eyes. "I'm not that much of a cliché."

Now it was Jack's turn to make a face. "You've got a very interesting personality."

"Right back at you."

Jack turned his attention back to his screen. "I'm not sure where else to go to look for answers on these symbols," he said, trying to return the focus of the conversation to the case. "I just can't find them anywhere online. I've gone to a bunch of different sites – anything even remotely related to pagan symbols – and I have nothing."

"I have a suggestion for that if you're interested in listening," Brian said.

Jack waited.

"You should show them to a witch."

Brian fought to keep his mouth from twitching when he saw Jack shift uncomfortably in his seat. He couldn't decide if it was excitement or dread fueling the man. Both were interesting options, though.

"You think I should show these to Ivy Morgan?" Jack asked. "How is she possibly going to be able to help?"

"I'm not sure that she can," Brian admitted. "She's still the best option we have. Instead of sitting here and spinning your wheels you should at least open yourself up to the possibility that Ivy might be able to help."

Jack frowned, rubbing the back of his neck as he considered how to proceed. "I actually took the photos out to her place last night," he said. "I already considered she might be able to identify the symbols."

"Oh," Brian said, disappointed. "She didn't recognize any of them?"

"I didn't get the chance to ask her," Jack said, wrinkling his nose. "She was … otherwise engaged."

"I'm going to need more information to know what you mean by that."

"She was with her boyfriend," Jack said. "I didn't feel like interrupting them. They seemed to be having a good time."

Brian furrowed his brow, confused. "What boyfriend? Last time I checked Ivy didn't have a boyfriend." He was pretty sure she hadn't had a boyfriend in years.

"I don't know who it was," Jack said. "He was a tall guy, a little over six feet if I had to guess. He had dark hair and he was well built. They spent some time in the yard talking and then they took off in the woods together. I'm guessing they were going for a walk."

"You spied on them?" Brian was starting to enjoy himself.

"I went out to take a look at the crime scene again, and I was hoping Ms. Morgan would be able to identify the symbols," Jack said. "Once I saw the … good time … she was having with her boyfriend, I didn't want to interrupt them. Although, now that I think about it, we should probably find out who her boyfriend is and question him."

Brian smirked. "I'll get right on that."

"You don't seem to think he's a suspect," Jack said. "Do you know who he is?"

"It sounds like Max," Brian said, unruffled.

"Who is Max? How long have they been dating?"

Brian stilled, Jack's question taking him by surprise. He knew very well who the man visiting Ivy Morgan was. It was the only man Ivy ever allowed to spend time with her these days. Maxwell Morgan was a former football stud and a genuinely nice guy. He was boisterous, and he worked his way through Shadow Lake's female population faster than any one man should be allowed to do. He was also loyal to his sister, and the idea of her finding a dead body on her property would naturally send him into a tailspin.

Max's appearance at Ivy's house wasn't cause for concern. Jack's nose being out of joint because he thought Max was Ivy's boyfriend was interesting, though. Brian decided to continue the charade. "I'm not sure how long they've been together," he said. "I just know they're close. Up until now I thought it was platonic."

"It's definitely not platonic," Jack said, inadvertently scowling.

"How do you know that?"

"They were ... flirting."

"Define flirting."

"They were talking in the yard and he chased her down and grabbed her and swung her around," Jack said. "If that's not flirting, I don't know what it is. There's no other explanation."

There was one. "Well, I'll track it down," Brian said. "While I'm handling that, why don't you run out to Morgan's Nursery and ask Ivy to look at the photos. She still might be able to identify the symbols."

Jack blanched. "Can't you do that?"

"I'm working on identifying the victim," he said. "I'm also handling the Max situation. You can do a little work."

Jack scowled, hating that his earlier jab was being thrown right back at him. "I'll do a little more work on the computer first," he said. "I'm not ready to give up."

"Suit yourself," Brian said, waiting until his back was turned to roll his eyes. "When you get tired of banging your head against a brick wall, though, you should know Ivy spends most of her time in the afternoon in the greenhouse."

"Thanks for the tip."

"You're welcome."

TWO HOURS LATER JACK WAS READY TO ADMIT DEFEAT. HE'D been clicking through an endless stream of websites promoting themselves as "one stop shops" of the pagan variety. Not one of them had the symbols he was looking for. He was ready to give in and visit Ivy Morgan. He didn't care how uncomfortable their interaction would be.

Now he just had to find a way to gracefully exit without Brian making fun of him. When Jack lifted his eyes he found Brian studying him.

"Are you ready to go see Ivy now?"

Jack sighed. "I don't have a lot of choice in the matter, do I?"

"There's always a choice, son," Brian said.

Then how come it doesn't feel that way? Jack ran a hand through his hair, frustrated. "I guess I'm going out to the nursery."

"I think that's a solid idea." Brian turned his attention back to the file, feigning seriousness. The smile tugging at the corner of his mouth gave him away, though.

"You're loving this, aren't you?"

"I'm loving it a little," Brian admitted. "I ... ."

Whatever else he was going to say was cut short when the door to the small detectives' office pushed open and Ava made her way in. She had a bright smile on her face and a pie platter in her hands.

Jack shifted in his chair, confused as his gaze bounced between Brian and Ava. *What is going on here?*

"Hello, gentleman," Ava said, beaming. "How are you this fine spring day?"

"Working," Brian said, not bothering to hide his scowl.

Ava ignored him. "How are you, Jack? Are you lonely yet? I'm betting you are. It must be hard not to know anyone in our small hamlet."

"I'm actually quite busy," Jack said.

"Oh, really? Doing what?"

"Well, I'm working on my house," Jack said. "There's a lot that needs to be done. I'm unpacking. Oh, and there's the murder that popped up yesterday afternoon."

Jack couldn't explain his immediate dislike for Ava, but he'd known she was going to be an annoying problem thirty seconds into their first conversation. She hadn't risen in his estimation since.

Ava slipped the pie platter onto the corner of Jack's desk, not letting his harsh tone ruffle her in the least. "That sounds really boring," she said. "Do you know what you need?"

Jack had a feeling she was going to tell him.

"You need a night on the town," Ava said. "The first barn dance of the season is going to be held this weekend. I thought you might want to go with me – just as friends, of course – and that way I could introduce you to more of the townspeople."

"Um … ." Jack glanced at Brian for help, but the older cop was pretending to focus on the file in front of him. Jack knew he was absorbing every word. "That's a very nice offer," he said finally. "I'm not much of a dancer, though. Also, a dance just isn't my scene."

"Oh, well, we don't have to go to the dance," Ava said. "We could go out to dinner instead. I could introduce you to people at the diner."

"I don't think that's going to work either," Jack said, debating how to handle the situation. She'd prefaced the invitation by stressing the "friends" part of the equation. If he pointed out he wasn't into dating he would risk not only alienating her – which he would be okay with – but embarrassing her, too. If Jack had learned anything over his thirty years it was that embarrassing a woman was more dangerous than calling her fat. "I have a really full plate right now. I don't have time for any nights out. Maybe … in a few weeks." It was never going to happen, but Jack would figure a way around that little problem when it popped up again. "I just really need to focus on my job and my house right now."

"And Ivy Morgan," Brian said, winking at Jack for good measure. "Don't forget you need to go and talk to her."

It was both a helpful suggestion and a way to get a dig in at Ava. Jack knew that. He still couldn't stop himself from being grateful for Brian's intervention. "I almost forgot," Jack said, pushing himself away from his desk and standing. "I need to get out to Morgan's Nursery."

Ava narrowed her eyes. "Why would you need to go back out there?"

"I just have a few more questions for Ms. Morgan," Jack replied evasively. "The victim was found on her property, after all."

"You know she's a witch, right?"

"I've been apprised of the situation," Jack replied, nodding.

"She's evil," Ava said. "If you're not careful, she'll cast a spell on you and make you fall in love with her. She did it all through high school. It's very … serious."

Jack forced his face to remain placid as he met Ava's serious gaze. "You don't have to worry about me falling in love with Ivy Morgan," he said, internally smiling when he realized he had the exact opening he was looking for. "I don't want a relationship. It's the last thing I want. She can try to cast a spell, but something tells me I'm going to be immune."

Ava relaxed her shoulders, but her face was still tense. "Well, I'm sure you'll change your mind once you're settled. I don't mean you should change your mind about Ivy, but once things are more … relaxed … I'm sure you'll be able to date someone else."

The smile Jack sent Ava was rueful. "Not even then," he said. "I'm just not the relationship sort. There's nothing that's going to change that." *Especially you,* he added silently before shifting his eyes to Brian. "I'll call you if I find anything."

Brian grinned. "Take your time. I'm sure Ivy will be a … gracious … hostess. She always is."

"Thanks," Jack said, moving toward the door.

"Be careful," Ava called to his retreating back. "She's a witch. You might not see it if she casts a spell on you."

"I'm sure I can handle Ivy Morgan," Jack said. "She's just a woman, after all."

Six

❦

Even though he'd been out to Ivy's house twice now, Jack paid little attention to the nursery that abutted her property on both visits. While you could walk from the cottage to the nursery without much problem – other than a short jaunt through the woods – the driveway to the nursery was only accessible via another road.

Jack took his time while parking, scanning the wide expanse with interested eyes and a resigned countenance. He was not going to enjoy this. Not only was he going to have to ask the woman for help, but he was probably going to have to listen to her gush about her boyfriend, too.

That sounded like an annoying way to spend an afternoon. Still … he didn't have a lot of options. He needed answers, and as far as he could tell, Ivy Morgan was the only one who could give them to him.

Jack took a meandering path through the nursery, stopping to study the myriad of trees and bushes as he moved through the facility. When Brian said she boasted the best stock in the area, he wasn't lying. The trees and bushes were robust, and Jack wasn't doubtful he'd stock up on items when he was ready to start landscaping at his own house.

"Are you shopping for anything in particular?"

Jack jumped when he heard Ivy's voice, forcing his face to remain even as he swiveled to face her. Like the day before, she was wearing an ankle-length skirt. This one was pink, matching her hair, and the simple black tank top she was wearing to offset the skirt was tight enough to highlight what Jack assumed was a terrific body.

Don't think about that, he chided himself. *What is wrong with you?*

"Hi," he said, hating how breathy he sounded. "I … um … how are you?"

Ivy lifted an eyebrow, her face caught between amusement and confusion. "I'm good. How are you?"

"Good," Jack said, rubbing his hands together nervously. "I … um … I'm good." *Get a grip.* He blew out a heavy sigh. "I'm fine. I just have something I need you to look at."

"Okay," Ivy said, amiable. "What is it?"

Jack glanced around at her customers, leery. There weren't a lot of them milling about, but this definitely wasn't something he wanted to show her in front of them. "Is there somewhere a little more private we can talk?"

Ivy's face shifted. "This is obviously about the body. Do you know who she is?"

"Not yet," Jack said. "We know she's not local, but that's about it right now. We're waiting for autopsy results, and we're hoping to get a hit on her fingerprints. If she doesn't have a record, we're going to have to figure out who she is another way."

"That's terrible," Ivy said. "Someone has to be missing her."

"I'm sure they are."

"I guess I don't understand," Ivy said. "If you're not here about the body, then why are you here? Are you … shopping?"

Jack chuckled, rubbing the back of his neck wearily. "Not yet. I have plans to get some stock when I get my house in better shape, but I'm nowhere near that point yet. I have to make sure the house doesn't fall down around me before I do anything else."

"I heard you bought the old Winstead house," Ivy said. "I've always loved that parcel. It's got great access to the lake. It's too bad the house is so run down."

"That's why I have to work on it."

"You're going to do all the work yourself?" Ivy looked surprised.

"Don't tell me you're another country person who thinks a city person can't do anything but call someone else to fix things," Jack said, his tone light and teasing. "That would be a disappointment."

Ivy tilted her head to the side, considering. "You're right. That's really not fair. I apologize."

"I accept your apology."

Ivy smirked, the gallant tone of his voice making her chuckle. "Not that I'm not happy to see you, but what are you doing here?"

"I have some photos of the ... body," Jack said carefully. "I need you to look at them."

Ivy took a step back, horrified. "What? Why?"

Now Jack was the apologetic one. "Someone ... carved ... some symbols into her body. I don't recognize them, and I've spent hours on the computer looking for some hint as to what they mean. I can't find anything. Brian suggested you might be able to help."

"How does he think I'll be able to help?"

Jack shifted uncomfortably. "The symbols look ... occult. Or maybe pagan. I'm not sure if there's a difference."

Ivy's face turned from open and concerned to dark and angry. "You naturally assumed I would be able to recognize occult symbols? It's because I'm a witch, right?"

"At least you call it like you see it."

Jack swiveled so he could study the approaching woman, keenly aware of the shift in Ivy's body language. The woman was pretty, long dark hair fluttering past her shoulders and offsetting a wide set pair of green eyes. She was wearing some of the tiniest shorts Jack had ever seen outside of a Detroit club, and the halter top she was wearing was cut so low she was almost showing everything she had off to anyone who happened to be looking.

"Maisie," Ivy said, biting her bottom lip. "I didn't see you standing there. How are you?"

"I need some bushes," Maisie said.

"Do you know what kind you want?"

"Not yet."

"Well … look around," Ivy said. "When you know, I'll be more than willing to help you."

"I know how it works," Maisie said, making a face. Now that Jack knew who she was, he was having a hard time swallowing his smile. Her reputation was obviously earned through hard work. She couldn't look more desperate if she tried. "I just want to say hello to Shadow Lake's newest citizen first. Unless you object, of course."

"I don't object," Ivy said. "You're welcome to … say hello … to anyone you want."

Jack let his gaze bounce between the two women. There was obviously some female competition going on here. He was certain he was at the center of it, although he couldn't decide if Ivy was engaging because she didn't want Maisie to lay claim to Shadow Lake's most recent transplant or if she was just arguing to argue. Maisie looked like the type of woman who ticked people off just by talking to them, and Ivy looked like the type of woman who liked to fight just because she could.

Jack extended his hand. "It's nice to meet you."

"It's really nice to meet you," Maisie purred, sidling up to him.

Ivy made a disgusted sound in the back of her throat, and when Jack lifted his eyes to hers he couldn't hide his smile. She had a beautiful face, and even when she was mad she practically glowed with an inner light he couldn't put a name to.

"I'm very happy to meet all the residents of Shadow Lake," Jack said, reluctantly tearing his eyes from Ivy's face. "I'm actually looking forward to it."

"I'm sure you are," Maisie said, running her finger up and down Jack's arm. "You're just … very handsome."

Jack's cheeks burned under Maisie's studied attention. "That's quite possibly flattering."

"It was meant to be flattering."

"Well … great."

"Do you have plans for lunch?" Maisie asked.

Jack glanced back at Ivy, hoping she would step in and help him. Instead, he found her face immovable as she watched the scene. It looked like he was on his own. "I do have plans for lunch," he said. "I'm working."

"If you're working, why are you out here?"

"I need some … help … from Ms. Morgan."

Maisie made a face, looking Ivy up and down as if sizing her up. "What kind of help?"

"The official kind I can't talk about," Jack said. "I'm sure you understand. We're working on a murder, and I can't let any of the details slip out to the general populace."

"But you can to Ivy?"

"The body was found on her property."

Maisie narrowed her eyes, considering. Finally, she must have decided Jack was telling the truth because she backed off. "Well, when you're ready to take me up on my offer, you can find me at the library."

"I'll keep that in mind."

Jack and Ivy watched Maisie shuffle away, refusing to pick their conversation back up until they were sure she was out of earshot.

"Um … what was I saying?" Jack asked.

"You were about to tell me that – since I'm a witch – I know every evil symbol in the world," Ivy said, crossing her arms over her chest.

Jack pursed his lips. "I'm pretty sure that's not what I was going to say."

"I'm pretty sure you were."

"Listen, I don't want to fight with you," Jack said, internally acknowledging that the last thing he wanted to do was argue with the comely greenhouse proprietor. "I really just thought you might be able to help. I don't know what I'm looking at. That's not easy for me to admit."

Ivy rolled her eyes and sighed, shifting from one foot to the other before reaching for the file. "Let me see."

"They're graphic."

Ivy's face paled. "I … understand."

"I've taken any with her face out. These are just the close ups. I'm … sorry."

Ivy widened her eyes. "Why? Are you the one who killed her."

"No."

"Did you dump her body in my ditch?"

"No."

"Then what do you have to be sorry about?" Ivy asked.

"This isn't your problem," Jack said, fighting the urge to reach over and brush the strand of flyaway hair away from her face. "I feel guilty asking you to look at these photos."

"Detective Harker … ."

"Call me Jack."

"Jack," Ivy said, tilting her head to the side. "I understand that you probably think I'm weak … and weird … and freaky. You would be right on two of those fronts. I am weird, and I am freaky. I'm not weak, though.

"That woman was found in front of my house," she continued. "I can't help but feel guilty. I'm worried she died one hundred feet from wherever I was sitting and I had the power to save her."

Jack's face softened. She was so … earnest. She was tough, but she had a gooey, soft center that managed to touch him in a place he'd long thought unavailable. "I think that believing you could've saved her is going to haunt you," he said. "You're better off believing you can help find her murderer."

"Are you sure she was murdered?"

"There were symbols carved into her body and she was stabbed," Jack said. "She was murdered."

Ivy's chest tightened. "I … hate this," she admitted, pinching the bridge of her nose. "I hate that there's so much hate in this world. I know that sounds ridiculous, but it's how I feel."

"I think a lot of people feel that way."

Ivy nodded. "Let me see the photos."

Jack handed them over wordlessly, watching her face as she studied them. She paled at the first one, and by the time she got to the tenth Jack was worried she was going to pass out. After flipping through them one more time, Ivy finally lifted her eyes to his. "I'm not sure."

"It's okay," he said.

"I don't need you to bolster me," Ivy said. "I'm aware that this is a disappointment to you. What I can say is that there's something familiar about the symbols. I just can't figure out what."

"Well, maybe if you give it some time … ."

"Maybe," Ivy replied. "I have some books I can look through, and I might have some other places to look. I … can I keep these for a few days?"

Jack balked, unsure. "If someone was to see those … ."

"I won't show anyone. I promise."

Jack relaxed, but only marginally. "That includes your boyfriend."

Ivy made a face. "What boyfriend?"

Jack held up his hands in an effort to placate her. "I saw you two here in the yard last night," he said. "I know you lied about having a boyfriend. It's not my concern. You can't show him these photographs, though."

"You were spying on me?"

"I … wanted to see the crime scene again," Jack said, stumbling over his words.

"Why didn't you say something? Why did you spy on me?"

"I wasn't spying," Jack said. "I was … thinking in my truck and I saw you with your boyfriend. I don't understand why you're freaking out about this."

"Clearly," Ivy said, crossing her arms over her chest.

"Hey, I'm not the one who lied," Jack said. "I could arrest you for lying to law enforcement. I think I'm being pretty generous here."

Ivy narrowed her eyes, pressing the file closer to her chest before opening her mouth. "I'm still going to figure out what these symbols mean," she said. "I'm not doing it to help you, though."

"I didn't ask you to help me," Jack snapped, irrational anger taking over.

"Whatever," Ivy said. "I'm doing this to help that girl. I don't appreciate your attitude, and I really don't appreciate you spying on me. My … relationships … are none of your concern. Now, when I know something, I will call Brian and tell him. There's no need for *you* to come back out here."

"That's a great way to run a business," Jack said snidely. "And, by the way, I wasn't spying."

Ivy didn't believe him. "Tell Brian I'll be in touch. As for yourself … have a nice life."

"Right back at you." Jack stalked off without a backward glance. He couldn't believe he ever thought she was hot.

Seven

"How did it go?"

Jack glanced up from the hamburger he was eating at his desk and fixed Brian with a weary look. "She's going to check her books."

"You don't sound very hopeful with the prospect of her figuring out what the symbols mean," Brian said, studying Jack quietly.

"She's got quite the attitude on her."

Brian smirked. "She always has," he said. "I think it has something to do with the fact that everyone always thought she was weird when she was growing up. A lot of the kids made fun of her."

Jack knew he should feel sorry for Ivy, but after her angry words he was having trouble mustering the energy. "Did they make fun of her because she was different, or did they go after her because she was ... bitchy?"

"She's not bitchy," Brian said, chuckling. "What did she do to you to get you in this state?"

"She accused me of spying on her."

Brian shifted, his face brightening. "I'm taking it you brought up her time with Max last night."

"I just asked her not to show the photographs to her boyfriend," Jack said. "I told her I wasn't going to arrest her for lying to law enforcement, even though I would totally be in my rights, and she just … flipped out. I have no idea why she's hiding that boyfriend, but he's obviously up to no good if she's so desperate to keep him a secret."

Brian pursed his lips, fighting the urge to laugh. Ivy clearly hadn't gotten around to telling Jack that Max was her brother – not her boyfriend – and he wasn't going to be the one to do it for her. He was kind of interested to see what would happen if Jack was left to his own devices. He was obviously attracted to Ivy. The question was: Would he acknowledge it? "I see. Did you leave the photos with her?"

"I did."

"What did she say?"

"She said that she would call you if she figured anything out. Then she banned me from her property."

Ah, there it is. Jack was agitated because Ivy eradicated the easiest way for him to see her. Brian couldn't help but wonder if Jack realized why he was reacting this way to Ivy and her fiery attitude. Something told him the boy was in denial – about more than one thing.

"Well, that will be fine," Brian said. "I like taking to Ivy. I've always found her delightful."

"That's probably because you haven't spent enough time with her," Jack snapped.

Brian swallowed his lower lip, nodding as he tamped down his laughter. "I'm sure that's it. Why don't you go home and get some sleep? We'll approach this from a new direction tomorrow."

"Are you sure?"

"I'm sure," Brian said. "Get some sleep. Hopefully, we'll have something new tomorrow. If we don't, we're just going to keep spinning our wheels here."

AFTER TOSSING AND TURNING MOST OF THE NIGHT, JACK woke up with a new idea and improved resolve. He didn't need Ivy Morgan to solve the mystery of the symbols. He just needed someone who understood what he was looking for and could think outside the box.

In other words: Ivy Morgan was not the only witch in the area.

After scouring the white pages online, Jack found exactly what he was looking for: The Magic Bag. It was a pagan store in neighboring Bellaire, and the Internet ad promised "supplies for all your magical needs."

To Jack, that sounded like an invitation.

By the time he parked in front of the kitschy store a lot of Jack's bravado had slipped. He knew that letting his anger with Ivy get the better of him wasn't a good idea. He also knew that trying to get all of the answers – and as quickly as possible – was part of being a good cop.

He couldn't solve Ivy's attitude problem. He could try and solve this case, though. That was his highest priority.

A set of wind chimes next to the front door served as an alert system for the owner. Even though Jack made noise upon entry, the woman behind the counter didn't bother looking in his direction.

"I'll be right with you, detective."

Jack froze, surprised. How could she possibly know who he was? He hadn't called ahead. He hadn't told anyone he was coming, including Brian. He'd sent the older detective a text message saying that he was checking on a lead and then promised to check in later. There was no way this woman could know who he was.

Jack took the opportunity to study her, swallowing the urge to snicker when he saw she was wearing a skirt that was very similar to the ones Ivy wore. It fell to a spot just above the woman's feet, and Jack was relieved to see she was wearing sandals. Instead of bright pink hair – and a fiery attitude – this woman was older. Jack pegged her age to be in the mid-fifties, and her dark hair – shot through with streaks of gray – was pulled back in a loose bun at the nape of her neck.

After a few minutes of uncomfortable silence, the woman turned her attention from the ledger she was balancing and finally focused on Jack. "I'm Felicity Goodings. How can I be of service?"

Now that she was finally acknowledging him, Jack was at a loss for how to approach her. He decided honesty was the best way to go. "How did you know I was a detective?"

Felicity smiled, the expression warming her round face. "I just … had a feeling. Was I wrong?"

Jack shook his head. "No. I can't help but feel like you were purposely trying to knock me off my game, though."

"That's not a very nice thing to say," Felicity said, her eyes twinkling.

"I'm sorry," Jack said, instantly apologetic.

"I didn't say you were wrong."

Jack returned her smile. "Well, at least you're honest."

"I don't know any other way to be," Felicity said. "What can I do for you?"

"I need some help," Jack said. "We had a murder in Shadow Lake the other night, and someone … a very bad person … carved some symbols into the victim's skin. I can't think of any other way to describe them besides occult, and I'm hoping you will be able to look at them and tell me if I'm on the right track.

"Just for the record, I'm not accusing you of being evil and I'm not insinuating all of this is evil," he continued, gesturing toward the store shelves. "I just don't know where else to look. I've been all over the Internet. I don't know what else to do."

Felicity smiled. "Well … that was a mouthful."

Jack pursed his lips, nodding. "Yes, it was. I got an earful from a local woman yesterday who accused me of some … not nice things … and I wanted to clarify that I am not out to malign anyone."

"That's very nice of you," Felicity said. "I'm not overly sensitive, though. Do you have photos of these symbols for me to look at."

Jack nodded. "They're … graphic."

"I figured they would be," Felicity said. "I can look at them. I understand the gravity of solving this case. This is a peaceful area, and the last thing we want is something like this to go on when it's not necessary."

Jack sighed, relieved. "Thank you for helping."

"I'm not promising I *can* help," Felicity cautioned. "I am

promising I *want* to help, though. So, how about you show me those photos and we go from there?"

"Yes, ma'am."

"I CAN'T SAY THAT I KNOW WHAT THESE ARE," FELICITY SAID, turning a few of the photos sideways so she could focus on them from another direction.

"What can you say?" Jack asked, lifting a candle and studying it before returning it to the shelf. "Do you think they mean something?"

"They obviously mean something," Felicity said. "You don't carve symbols into someone's body if it doesn't mean something. The question is: Do they mean something to more than one person?"

"I'm not sure I understand," Jack replied honestly.

"One man can convince himself there's power in a symbol, even if he makes it up himself," Felicity explained. "Multiple men can find power in a symbol if it means something to more than one person."

"That kind of sounds like a riddle."

"It's not meant to," Felicity said. "There is something very familiar about these symbols. I just can't figure out where I've seen them before."

"Believe it or not, you're not the first person to tell me that," Jack said.

"Who else have you shown these to?"

"There's a local woman in Shadow Lake," Jack said. "I'm new to the area, and my partner suggested I take the photos to her. The body happened to be found on her property, so I thought she would be willing to help."

Felicity made a face. "She wasn't?"

"She was," Jack said. "She just ... has an attitude where I'm concerned. I'm not sure what I did to her, but she doesn't want to help me. She wants to help the dead woman, and I don't want to act like she's not willing to help when she is. I'd just rather get someone else to give me some insight if I can.

"It's not easy to get a lead when the person with the answers won't talk to you," he said.

Felicity's smile was small but heartfelt. "This woman … did she give you any indication why she was so angry with you?"

"I think she just hates men."

Felicity wrinkled her nose, confused. "I see."

"I don't think you do," Jack said. "She's … belligerent."

"Many men say that about many women."

"No, this woman is really mean. I thought she was just nervous as first. That's definitely not the case, though."

"Maybe she thinks you're … belligerent … too."

"I don't see how that's possible," Jack said. "I've been nothing but professional and friendly."

"Well, I still think it's probably a misunderstanding," Felicity said. "Do you mind if I scan some of these photos into my computer? I have a program that will match them to any reference materials I have on my laptop. It might take some time, but it will cut down on the legwork."

Jack nodded. "Go for it."

"It will just take me a second," Felicity said, gathering the photos to her chest and turning to the back of the store. "Make yourself at home. Look around. I won't be long."

"You're helping me," Jack said. "Take as long as you need."

"There's tea in the pot over there," Felicity said, pointing. "Help yourself. I'll be right back."

Once Felicity disappeared into the back room, Jack busied himself by studying the shelves. He wasn't sure what to expect in a magic store, but the items on the shelves seemed tame compared to his runaway imagination.

There were candles, crystals, incense and books. There was also a whole wall of wind chimes and dreamcatchers, the latter being an item Jack recognized from his childhood. He was often plagued by bad dreams. His mother bought a dreamcatcher at a local fair and put it over his bed, telling him it would catch the nightmares before they could lodge in his brain.

At such a young age, Jack believed her. After seeing the things he'd seen, though, he knew that wasn't the case. He still liked the look of them. He was moving closer so he could study them when the door to the store opened. He turned, ready to tell the customer that Felicity would be back in a moment, but the greeting froze on his lips when he realized who was walking through the door.

The woman's blue eyes registered surprise when they landed on him.

"Just what do you think you're doing here?" Ivy asked.

Eight

Jack was taken aback. "What are you doing here?"

Ivy glowered at him. "I asked you first."

"I was here first, so I have dibs on the question."

"That's not how it works," Ivy said, placing her hands on her narrow hips as she regarded him. She was dressed differently today, a pair of slouchy cargo pants hanging just low enough that a small strip of skin was visible between the top of the pants and the bottom of her sparkly tank top. The cargo pants were rolled up, and Ivy's toned calves jutted out above the Nike flip-flops she was sporting. The whole package was appealing – if you liked that sort of thing. And he didn't like that sort of thing, Jack reminded himself.

Well, at least she's wearing shoes this time, Jack internally muttered. "I'm ... looking for information on my case."

"Here? You're looking for information here?"

"I need to know what those symbols mean," Jack said, crossing his arms over his chest. "I'm sure you understand – given your *attitude* yesterday – I wasn't sure if you would come through. I needed to find someone else who might be able to help."

"My attitude?"

"That's what I said."

"You're the spy."

"I was not spying!"

"What's going on out here?" Felicity wandered back to the front of her shop, her gaze bouncing between Ivy and Jack curiously. "You two sound like you should be in a boxing ring instead of a store."

"I'm sorry," Jack said, immediately apologetic. "That was incredibly rude."

Felicity focused on Ivy.

"I'm not sorry at all," Ivy said, nonplussed. "He's a pain."

"I see you two know each other," Felicity said, handing Jack his stack of photographs and slipping between the warring duo so she could give Ivy a brief hug. "I'm guessing this is the woman you were telling me about earlier."

Jack made a face as he watched the women embrace. "Something tells me you knew I was talking about her all along." He was starting to feel as if he was caught in a trap.

"I had a feeling," Felicity said, smiling at him. "I only know two witches in Shadow Lake, and something told me that you weren't fighting with Luna."

"And Luna is your mother, right?" Jack asked, glancing at Ivy.

"I'm sure you found that out while you were spying," Ivy snapped.

"Ivy Morgan! That will be just about enough of that," Felicity said, waving her finger in the younger woman's face. "I don't allow anyone to treat customers that way in my store."

"He's not a customer," Ivy shot back, refusing to give in. "He's here to get information even though I already told him I would get it for him."

"After you banned me from your property."

"Because you were spying."

"How many times do I have to tell you I wasn't spying?"

"Just until you believe it," Ivy seethed.

Felicity held her hands up to silence them both. "Okay … I just … wow. There is so much energy zipping through this room I'm afraid you two are going to start a fire. Let's start from the beginning, what's going on?"

"Nothing is going on," Jack answered, squaring his shoulders. "We just have a difference of opinion."

"He was spying on me the day before yesterday," Ivy said. "He sat in his truck and hid while watching me."

"What were you doing?" Felicity asked.

"Nothing."

"I was not spying on you," Jack said, feeling increasingly irrational. "I was looking over the spot where the body was found. I just happened to see you with your boyfriend. Since you told me you didn't have a boyfriend while I was questioning you, I just found it suspicious."

Felicity arched an eyebrow. "Since when do you have a boyfriend?"

"He's talking about Max," Ivy said.

"I see." Felicity glanced between the two glowering faces for a moment, deciding there was only one way to solve this little dilemma. "Everyone meet me in front of the store. We're going to lunch."

"I'm not here for lunch," Ivy protested. "I'm here to talk to you about those symbols."

"And Jack wants to talk about them, too," Felicity said. "I loaded them into my computer and the search is running, but it's going to take some time. While we're waiting, we're all going to lunch together."

"I'm not really hungry," Jack said. "I'm fine waiting here."

"Me, too," Ivy said, wrinkling her nose.

"Well, I'm hungry," Felicity said. "I'm not leaving you two in here to yell at each other for an hour. You're both coming with me. I don't want to hear one argument."

"But … ." Jack broke off, unsure. It appeared there was no way out of this situation.

"I don't want to," Ivy said, pouting.

"You're going, Ivy," Felicity said. "Don't make me physically drag you out of this store."

"Oh, Auntie."

Auntie? Jack realized the new informational tidbit made sense. Of course they were related. If he didn't have bad luck he would have no luck at all.

. . .

"ISN'T THIS NICE?" FELICITY ASKED, GRINNING WIDELY AS SHE glanced between Ivy and Jack. They'd settled on a local diner that boasted some of the finest vegetarian fare in town, and after ordering, Jack and Ivy were now taking turns shooting glares at one another across the table.

Felicity knew her niece well enough to know what was going on, even though she didn't think she'd live long enough to actually see it. She didn't know Jack at all, but she could see the same emotional turmoil rolling off him in waves.

There was enough sexual attraction manifesting between the two of them you could almost cut it with a knife. Since neither one of them wanted to deal with it they were letting the baser part of their personalities do it for them. In other words: They were acting like children.

"It's great," Ivy said sarcastically.

"Listen, young lady, you're being incredibly rude," Felicity said. "I happen to know this is not the way you were raised. Don't make me have a talk with your mother."

Ivy stuck her tongue out. "She's still not back in town."

"She'll be here very soon," Felicity replied. "She's my sister. We're in contact all the time. I have a very long memory. Enough is enough with you."

The look Jack shot Ivy was one of triumph.

"I wouldn't get too high on your horse," Felicity said, turning to him. "You're not acting much better. I know she knows better. I can't say the same for you."

Jack sighed. "I apologize. I think your niece just brings out the worst in me."

"I don't think that's the first time she's heard that," Felicity said. "Ivy, don't you have something to say to Jack?"

"I accept your apology."

Felicity kicked her under the table.

"Ow! Fine. I'm sorry, too."

"Thank you," Felicity said, turning her attention back to her iced tea.

"You still spied on me," Ivy said.

"I'm not going over this again," Jack warned. "I don't spy on people. I just happened to see you with your boyfriend."

Felicity was intrigued by the fact that Ivy refused to correct Jack's erroneous assumptions about Max. Was she trying to make him jealous? If so, it was working. Of course, Jack wasn't internally admitting he was jealous so he would never acknowledge it. His aura was red, but there was a dark gray at the center. That meant he was hurt, and if Felicity had to guess he'd been injured both physically and emotionally. The physical ailments were in the past. The emotional ones were still clawing at the surface. A softer pink hue was intermingling with the other layers, though, and that was because of Ivy. She was ... doing something to him.

"Okay, let's start over," Felicity said, deciding to change tactics. She had no intention of blabbing Ivy's secret, but she also wasn't going to let her niece torture Jack when he didn't deserve it. "Ivy, I'm sure Jack is sorry he spied on you and ... your boyfriend. Can't you just be the bigger person and forgive him?"

"I have the right to privacy in my own yard," Ivy said.

"You also had a dead body in your yard and Jack is a police officer," Felicity pointed out. "Don't you think he has a right to solve the crime?"

"I ... ."

Felicity cut her off. "Or are you so worried about yourself that you don't want a brutal murder to be solved?"

Ivy scowled. "That is ridiculous."

"I agree," Felicity said. "I think it's time you let it go."

"Fine," Ivy said, sighing dramatically. "I forgive you for spying on me. You're unbanned from my property. Just ... don't do it again."

"I'll try to refrain," Jack said dryly.

"You could be nicer," Felicity said, poking his strong shoulder and marveling at the muscles that rippled beneath his shirt. "I'm sure you understand that Ivy is feeling a little exposed. That's been her home for her entire life. She's always felt safe there. Now she feels ... vulnerable. And, if I know her, she's also feeling guilty. She's probably spent the past forty-eight hours wondering if there was something she could've done to save that girl. That's a lot to carry around."

Jack pressed the heel of his hand against his forehead, frustrated. "I'm sorry. I didn't really think about that. I just … I'm sorry."

"Good," Felicity said, brightening. "Apologies all around. Everyone can move on now."

Ivy grudgingly nodded. "I really am sorry. I shouldn't have been so mean to you. I just don't like the idea of people watching me. After finding the body … it just creeps me out."

"I should have taken that into consideration," Jack said. "I honestly wasn't spying. I was just trying to get a feel for the scene. I think better that way. I was trying to picture how the victim ended up there."

"It must be hard to be a police officer," Felicity said. "You've probably seen a lot."

The gray in Jack's aura flared, the hurt taking over. "I've seen more than my fair share."

That was obviously the truth. "Tell me about Detroit." Felicity couldn't help herself. Jack's vibes had a mind of their own, and the source of his turmoil revolved around something terrible that happened to him in the city.

Jack balked. "What are you talking about?"

Felicity ratcheted back her inner probe. "I'm sorry. That's none of my business. I shouldn't be delving into things you're not ready to talk about. What happened to you is … ."

"Nothing happened to me," Jack said, shifting in his chair angrily. "Who told you something happened to me in Detroit?"

"No one," Felicity said, holding her hand up. "I just … I sensed you were having some trouble. I'm sorry. I didn't mean to invade your privacy."

"You sensed I was having some trouble?" The dark glint in his eyes caused Felicity to inadvertently shudder as a quick flash of ravaging hate arced out from his soul.

Without even realizing what she was doing, Ivy reached across the table and wrapped her hand around Jack's wrist, drawing his attention to her. The air around them sparked, and Jack's eyes softened as they met Ivy's concerned face. The pink in his aura pushed in on the gray, tamping down the hurt he was so desperate to hide. "She doesn't mean anything by it. She just has … feelings about people. It's okay."

Jack nodded, momentarily mesmerized by Ivy's face. "I … ."

"This is a difficult thing for all of us to deal with. I know I've been … obnoxious. I'm sorry. No one is trying to upset you," Ivy said. "We all need to work together to find out who this girl is, and what happened to her."

Jack cleared his throat, the spell breaking as Ivy slowly retracted her fingers. "I'm sorry for … snapping at you. This whole case is … throwing me. Whenever I don't understand what's going on, I tend to get my hackles up. I think Ivy is right, though. We need to work together, not turn on each other."

"Okay," Felicity said, exhaling heavily. "Um … I think the best way to proceed is for me to see what I can find on the symbols. I'm sure you have other things you want to check out. I'll be in touch the second I find anything."

"Good," Jack said, rubbing the tender spot between his eyebrows. When he risked a look back in Ivy's direction, he found her eyes trained on him. Instead of the animosity he'd found there earlier, he saw nothing but softened interest flowing through her now. "I'll keep in touch with you, too."

Ivy forced a small smile for his benefit. "It's going to be okay. We'll figure it out."

Felicity couldn't hide her grin as she watched the interaction. It was if they were in their own little world. She couldn't help but wonder if that world would strengthen or crumble in the coming weeks. Personally, she was rooting for it to strengthen.

Jack Harker might just turn out to be the man her tempestuous niece needed to finally break through and touch her well-protected heart. Of course, Ivy might also be the person to soothe Jack's troubled heart – if he gave her the chance, that is.

It was certainly going to be entertaining to watch either way.

Nine

"Do you want to tell me what's going on?"

Ivy lifted her eyes from the book she was reading at Felicity's store counter and fixed a quizzical look on her face. "I have no idea what you're talking about."

After the computer search took longer than expected, and Jack and Ivy couldn't take another second of fighting the urge to touch one another, Shadow Lake's newest detective bid them farewell and promised to keep in touch. The second he left the store, Ivy's mood lifted.

"Oh, don't do that," Felicity said, smiling at her only niece. "You're like a daughter to me. I know when something is up with you. Something is definitely up with you."

"He just rubs me the wrong way."

Felicity snorted. "I think it's actually the opposite, but if you need to tell yourself that, then go ahead."

"Excuse me?"

"You're attracted to him," Felicity said, refusing to back down. "It's written all over your face."

"I think you read auras better than you do faces," Ivy replied, nonplussed.

"Your aura says it, too."

"Maybe you're just off your game today." Ivy focused back on the book. "I haven't found anything that helps us yet. How much longer do you think the computer search will take?"

She was trying to change the subject. There was no way Felicity was going to let that happen. "He's very handsome," Felicity said. "There's something rather pleasing about his face. I think it's that strong jaw of his."

"I guess," Ivy said, refusing to meet her aunt's probing gaze. "If you like that kind of thing."

Felicity couldn't help but grin. *Who didn't like that kind of thing?* "I touched his shoulder, too. He feels like he works out quite a bit."

"Maybe you should date him," Ivy suggested. "He's new in town. The vultures are circling, but if you move fast enough you can probably cut Ava and Maisie off at the knees and claim him for yourself."

"I think I'm a little old for him."

"Maybe that's what he likes."

"I think he likes you," Felicity said. There was no way she was going to let Ivy wriggle out of this conversation.

"Oh, good grief," Ivy said, rolling her eyes until they landed on her aunt. "We have spent a grand total of two hours together now. He doesn't know me. We've talked about a murder, he's spied on me, and I've yelled at him. That's the extent of our relationship."

"I didn't say you were in love with him," Felicity said. "I said you were attracted to him. Love is emotional. Attraction is physical. There's a big difference."

"I suppose you're going to enlighten me on the difference, aren't you?"

"You don't know him well enough to love him," Felicity said, ignoring the sarcasm. "That doesn't mean your skin doesn't hum whenever he's around. Don't bother denying it. I saw your auras touch when you grabbed his wrist. He was about to fly off the handle, and you managed to center him with a simple touch. It was … beautiful."

"I think you're reading a little more into our interaction than what is really there," Ivy said. "He just needed a second to collect himself.

You threw him off his game. You need to stop blurting stuff like that out, by the way. Some people don't like it."

"He's been through something truly horrible," Felicity said.

"How do you know that?" Despite herself, Ivy was interested. She'd sensed the same thing about Jack. She couldn't see auras like her aunt, but she trusted her instincts.

"He's been terribly hurt," Felicity said. "Part of it was physical. I didn't see a lot. He likes to hold his troubles close to his heart. He almost died, though. I did see that. And whoever was responsible for hurting him physically also betrayed him on a personal level. I don't know the specifics. I just know that he's a man who can't let go of something very bad."

"That makes me feel guilty," Ivy said. "I was pretty mean to him yesterday."

"That's what I heard."

"He had it coming, though," Ivy said. "I don't care what he says. He was spying on me."

Felicity pursed her lips. "First off, I don't think he was technically spying on you," she said. "I do think he wanted to check out the crime scene. I also think there's something about you that calls to him."

"Oh, whatever," Ivy grumbled.

"I want to know why you're letting him believe Max is your boyfriend."

"He jumped to that conclusion," Ivy said. "I'm not rewarding his spying by telling him the truth."

"Did you ever consider he jumped to that conclusion because he was jealous?"

"He just met me. We're not dating. He has nothing to be jealous about."

"If it's any consolation, I don't think he realizes he's jealous," Felicity said. "He's not looking for a relationship – just like you. He just has all these … feelings, for lack of a better word … and he has no idea what to do with them."

"He should figure out a different way to deal with them."

"I know someone else feeling the exact same thing," Felicity said pointedly.

Ivy slammed the book shut and hopped down from the stool. "And on that note … I'm going." She kissed her aunt on the cheek. "Call me when you find something. I can't put up with another second of your meddling."

"Is that because you know I'm right?"

"Auntie, Jack doesn't have feelings for me," Ivy said. "Even if he was attracted to me, we both know that wouldn't last for more than a few weeks before all the … witchy stuff … drove him away. I've gone through it too many times. I'm not going through it again."

"You don't know that he would walk away."

"Yes, I do," Ivy said. "I'm used to it. I know my lot in life. I'm fine being who I am. I'm fine being alone."

Felicity wasn't so sure, but she snapped her mouth shut and let Ivy keep whatever delusions she needed to cling to as she walked out of the store. She had no doubt this situation was going to explode. It was probably best to let Jack and Ivy deal with their feelings in their own time. It was the only way they were going to learn. Some things are inevitable, after all.

JACK WAS FRUSTRATED. HOURS OF RESEARCH TO FIND THE meaning of the symbols had proved fruitless – although he was sure Felicity was toiling away. Brian was still trying to track down the victim's identity, and until they knew who she was, there was no way they could figure out what to do.

He literally had nowhere to go in the investigation without more information.

After leaving the office, he drove home, visions of starting restoration on the front porch of his new house flitting through his head. He got exactly one hour of haphazard work done before he gave up. He couldn't focus on the house when there was so much about the murder left unexplained.

Who was she? Who killed her? What did the symbols mean? Why was her body dumped in front of Ivy Morgan's house? Was that just a coincidence?

The coroner put the time of death about nine hours before Ivy discovered the body. Due to the lack of blood on the ground beneath the woman – who was believed to be about nineteen years old – it was ascertained that she was killed elsewhere and dumped in the ditch. That was something. At least Ivy could let go of the guilt. There was nothing she could have done to save the woman. Of course, since the final autopsy report didn't hit his desk until right before he left, there was no way she could know.

Maybe I should tell her?

Jack had no idea where the idea came from, but the moment it occurred to him it was all he could think about. Ivy was troubled by the notion that she could have saved the woman. It was only fair to tell her that wasn't the case. It would help her sleep better.

Before he realized what was happening Jack was in his truck and on his way to Ivy's house. He would just stop in for a second, he told himself. He wasn't going to see her. He was going to make sure she knew what was going on. That was an important distinction. Besides, it would give him another chance to study the ditch. There was something there he was missing. He just knew it.

Instead of parking in front of Ivy's cottage, which would be a dead giveaway, Jack parked down the road and walked up the highway. He left the cracked pavement so he could traipse through the trees, studying the ground for signs of disturbance.

It made more sense for the murderer to have used a vehicle to discard the body than carrying dead weight through the woods. Ivy's house was set back from the road. Even if she was staring out the window at the exact moment the body was dumped, she wouldn't have seen a car on the road – especially if the lights were disengaged.

Jack emerged from the woods, landing on Ivy's driveway and shifting so he could take in the entire area as he turned. Why dump someone's body in front of a house when there was so much empty land surrounding it? If the murderer was trying to hide what he'd done, wouldn't it make more sense to pick a completely isolated spot? It was almost as if someone wanted the woman's body to be found. That couldn't be it, could it?

Jack was so lost in thought he didn't notice the furtive figure shooting toward him from the other side of the driveway until it was upon him.

"Oomph."

The figure was tall and built, and even though Jack worked out every day, he was no match for the interloper's fury or determination. Jack was already on the ground, his hands moving up to protect his face when he recognized who was on top of him. It wasn't some crazy madman – or, at least he didn't think so. No, this was a whole other level of annoyance. It was Ivy's boyfriend.

"Don't you even think about going near my sister!" Max slammed his fist into Jack's face.

IVY, HER HAND MOVING THROUGH NICODEMUS' SOFT FUR AS SHE flipped through a magazine, tensed out of nowhere. *Something is going on.* She shifted the cat, his angry cry ignored as she moved to the front door. Someone was outside. She had no idea how she knew, but she did.

Without thinking of the possible ramifications, Ivy threw open the door and scanned her small yard. Since the cottage was set back from the road, the trees hid its existence from prying eyes. There were plenty of places to hide, though.

The unmistakable sound of scuffling assailed Ivy's ears, and she turned her attention to the far end of the driveway where she saw two men grappling with one another. She didn't recognize the figure on the ground, but the one on top belonged to her brother. "Max?"

Max didn't look up. Whoever he was wrestling with was strong, and before her brother could secure him in a wrestling hold the other figure gained the upper hand and flipped Max over, toppling him to the ground.

Ivy broke into a run, her heart pounding as she raced toward the two men. If this was a dangerous situation, she might well regret intervening. Max was her brother, though. She would never abandon him.

By the time Ivy made it to the end of the driveway the second man managed to subdue Max and was holding his struggling body against the uncomfortable gravel. It took Ivy a second to recognize her visitor, but when she did, she couldn't contain her anger.

"You let him go right now!"

Jack shifted his eyes to Ivy, causing her to take an involuntary step back when she absorbed the full brunt of his emotional fury. "He attacked me."

"Let him go," Ivy said, keeping her voice firm. "That is my brother."

Jack faltered, letting his grip on Max loosen. He glanced down at the man on the ground, his eyes roaming over the familiar features. Now that she'd said it, Jack didn't understand how he hadn't recognized the family resemblance. Max was taller and broader, but they had the same eyes and bone structure. "I ... ."

Jack rolled off Max, taking a step back and raising his hands to ward off a second attack.

For his part, Max was mortified. He jumped to his feet and angrily started dusting his clothes off. "I caught him wandering around in the woods over there. I think he was going to attack you."

Ivy tilted her head to the side, conflicted. Was he spying again? "Why are you here, Jack?"

"Jack?" Max rolled the name through his mind. "Is this the new cop?"

Ivy nodded.

"Why are you stalking my sister, man?"

"This is your brother?" Jack asked, never moving his gaze from Ivy's expressive face.

"Yes."

"Why didn't you just tell me that?"

"I ... ." *Why hadn't she?* "I was mad at you. I wanted to bug you as much as you were bugging me."

Jack barked out a hoarse laugh, running his hand through his hair. "I guess I deserve that."

"Does someone want to tell me what's going on here?" Max asked, frustrated.

"I'm Jack Harker." Jack extended his hand by way of greeting, and Max reluctantly shook it. "I was just going through the woods over there because I wanted to make sure that no one carried the body to the ditch. I wasn't spying. I was just ... looking around."

Max exhaled heavily. "I ... I'm sorry. I jumped to conclusions. Ivy is all alone out here. When I saw a man I didn't know going through the woods by her house I thought ... well ... I think you know what I thought."

"You were trying to protect her," Jack said. "I get it. Don't worry about it."

"I didn't hurt you, did I?"

Jack rubbed his shoulder. "You knocked the wind out of me, but I'm fine. I didn't hurt you, did I?"

"You're freaking strong, man," Max said. "I see you did some wrestling back in the day. That was a nice move to flip me over."

"I see you did, too. You caught me completely off guard when you tackled me. I barely saw you coming."

Ivy rolled her eyes as the two men lapsed into a high school athletics conversation. It seemed the crisis had passed, even if she wasn't sure exactly what happened out here. What is it with men? They can beat the crap out of each other and then immediately get over it. That was not the way of the world where women were concerned.

Ten

"Why did you want to meet here?" Jack slid into the booth across from Brian and fixed the older man with a pointed look. "Shouldn't we be working?"

"What do you suggest we work on?" Brian asked, lifting an eyebrow as he sipped from his coffee mug. "We have no idea what the symbols represent, and we still don't have an identification on the victim. We have nothing."

"So … we're going to have breakfast?"

"I figured now would be a good time for you to meet some of the regulars," Brian said. "Plus, a solid breakfast never hurt anyone, and this place has the best breakfast in town. Although, you strike me as an oatmeal guy."

"Why do you say that?"

"Because you don't look like you eat a lot of greasy food," Brian said. "You look like one of those 'my body is my temple' guys."

Jack snorted. "That shows what you know."

"Did you eat breakfast this morning?"

"Yes."

"Was it oatmeal?"

"I had fruit with it, too," Jack replied, annoyed.

Brian grinned. "Try the eggs. They're amazing. They're fresh from a local farm."

"I'll consider it," Jack said, reaching for a menu. "So we still have nothing?"

"Absolutely nothing," Brian said, studying his new partner's face. "What happened to your cheek? It looks like you've been in a fight."

Jack's face burned under Brian's gaze. "I … um … had a thing last night."

"What was her name?"

Jack scowled. "*His* name was Max Morgan."

"I see you finally found out that Ivy's boyfriend was actually her brother," Brian said, chuckling. "How did that happen?"

"I was checking the woods by her house to see if there was any reason to suspect the victim was carried to the dump site instead of driven and he tackled me," Jack said.

"Why did he tackle you?"

"He thought I was there stalking his sister," Jack said. "I don't blame him. He had no idea who I was, and his sister lives alone. He was just protecting her."

"How did Ivy take all of this?"

"After a little yelling she was fine," Jack said. "She's kind of loud on a normal day, though, so she was especially loud yesterday."

"Hmm."

"What is that supposed to mean?" Jack asked, irritated.

"It doesn't mean anything," Brian said. "I just find it … interesting … that you found yourself at Ivy's house again. You seem to come up with reasons to be out there quite a bit these days."

"I don't need a reason," Jack said. "I think the dead body being discovered on the premises is plenty reason for me to want to look around the woods there."

"If that's your story … ."

"I don't have a story."

"Whatever," Brian said, exhaling heavily. "I've seen the way you look at Ivy. I'm not blaming you for it. She's an attractive woman. You might even have a shot with her. I've seen the way she looks at you, too. There's something there."

"I've already told you, I'm not looking to date anyone," Jack said. "I'm doing the best I can. I'm not interested in Ivy Morgan."

"That's good," Brian said, his eyes drifting toward the front of the restaurant.

"Are you going to let this go?"

"I am," Brian said. "Oh, um, she's heading this way."

Jack shifted quickly, glancing over his shoulder and internally sighing when he saw Ivy. Of course, because his luck continued to plummet, she wasn't alone. Her brother was with her. This morning just kept getting worse and worse.

"THERE'S your new friend," Max said, waving at Jack while waggling his eyebrows at Ivy. "I think it's fate."

"Shut up," Ivy said.

"Ivy and Jack sitting in a tree … ."

"I will beat the crap out of you," Ivy warned, wagging a finger in her brother's face. "You're being incredibly obnoxious."

"I learned it from you," Max said, focusing on the booth. "Come on."

"Where are we going?"

"We're going to sit with them."

"No, we're not."

Max ignored her and strode toward the booth. "Hey. Do you guys have room for two more?"

Before Jack could answer Brian immediately started sliding over in the booth. "Sure. That sounds good. We can do some brainstorming."

Max took the spot next to Brian, which meant Ivy had no choice but to slide in next to Jack. They looked at each other for a moment, uncertain, and then Jack edged over. "Have a seat," he muttered.

"Thank you," Ivy said. She was stiff as she settled next to him, but even though they were going out of their way to keep from the touching one another, the warmth radiating between them was hard to ignore. "I … um … how are you this morning?"

"I'm good," Jack said. "How are you?"

"I was great until a few minutes ago," Ivy said, glowering at Max.

Max ignored her and turned to Brian. "How's the farm?"

"It's good," Brian said. "We're getting ready to start the spring run up. We need to get everything planted in two weeks, so we're kind of behind."

"If you need help, I can come out," Max offered. "I haven't seen Sean and Simon in a couple months. It might be fun to hang out with them."

"I'll tell them," Brian said. "How is the lumber business?"

"Busy," Max said. "Spring is our busiest time of year, so we've had a lot of stuff delivered to the yard over the past week. It's pretty bustling."

"You work at a lumber yard?" Jack asked, suddenly interested. He had a lot of renovations in front of him.

"I own Morgan Lumber down on the highway," Max said. "I heard you bought the Winstead house. You're probably going to need supplies. If you need something, come out and ask for me. I'll give you a good deal. I figure I owe you after tackling you last night."

Brian grinned. "I heard about that. Who won?"

"It was a tie," Jack said, reaching for the mug of coffee the waitress was pushing in his direction.

"Jack won," Ivy said, sticking her tongue out at Max.

"I let him win," Max countered.

"Oh, whatever," Ivy scoffed. "If I hadn't run out to save you Jack would have beat you into a bloody pulp."

"Tell her that's not true," Max ordered, staring at Jack.

"It was a draw," Jack repeated.

Brian couldn't hide his snicker. "It sounds like you guys had some fun."

"Then I'm telling it wrong," Max said. "He scared the crap out of me. I thought for sure whoever killed that girl was back and he was going after Ivy."

"I'm fine," Ivy said. "I'm perfectly capable of taking care of myself."

"You're still alone out there, Ivy," Brian said. "You can't blame your brother for being worried about you. If you would get a dog like I asked … ."

"I have Nicodemus," Ivy said. "He's all the pet I need. He's an excellent watch cat."

"Yes, I love it when he watches the same spot – usually a shadow – on the wall and thinks it's a bug," Max said. "He's vicious."

"He attacks you all the time," Ivy pointed out.

"That's because I forget to tie my shoes and he thinks the laces are snakes. He's a real brainiac."

"Don't you talk bad about my cat," Ivy warned.

"Fine," Max said, leaning back in the booth. "Since you won't get a dog, though, I'm thinking it might be smart for you to come and stay with me for a couple of days."

"That's a good idea," Brian said.

"Absolutely not," Ivy said. "That is my home. I love that place. I'm not staying with you. Besides, I need to stick close to the nursery. This is our busy season, too."

"How did I know you were going to say that?" Max grumbled.

"Maybe you're psychic."

Max reached for her across the table, but she was too quick. In her haste to avoid her brother's outstretched hand, Ivy bumped into Jack. The second their skin touched they were both on fire. They jolted away from one another, scattering to opposite ends of the booth.

Max tilted his head to the side, wide-eyed as he watched them. He had no idea what happened, but it was definitely something. Jack and Ivy were desperate to keep from touching each other. Well, that was interesting.

"If you don't want to stay with me I'm probably going to have to move in with you," Max said after a moment. "Are you prepared for that?"

"I'll change the locks before that happens," Ivy said.

"Ivy, you're my sister," Max said. "As much as I really want to rub your face in my armpit until you cry right now, the truth is that I can't bear the thought of anything happening to you. I'm not sure you're safe out there alone."

"Your brother is right, Ivy," Brian said. "You're a pretty girl. If someone is after a woman who is isolated ... you'd be right on top of their list."

Ivy frowned. "Listen, I appreciate all the … hovering. I'm not leaving my home, though, and no one is moving in. Don't bother arguing, Max. You and I learned a long time ago that our personalities are too big to live under that roof together."

"That's because you're whiny," Max said.

"I am not whiny," Ivy said. "You're just a big … slobbering machine. You're worse than a dog."

"I don't slobber."

"Whatever," Ivy said.

Jack grinned at the banter. He couldn't help himself. Despite the mean words, it was obvious brother and sister loved each other very much. It made him look at Ivy in a completely different way – which caused his heart to somersault when he risked a glance in her direction. She really was lovely.

"Okay, if Ivy refuses any and all help – which is frankly her nature – that means we need to get a break on this case," Brian said. "I heard you both were out at Felicity's shop yesterday. Did you find anything?"

"You two went to Aunt Felicity's shop together?" This was news to Max.

"We went separately," Ivy said. "We just ran into each other."

"I heard you had a cozy lunch," Brian said, teasing his partner.

"Who told you that?" Jack asked, surprised.

"Felicity is friends with Millie," Brian replied, unfazed. "She called last night to gossip."

"W-w-what did they gossip about?" Jack was uncomfortable, but he couldn't put his finger on exactly why.

"Felicity just said you two were balls of energy who wouldn't stop sniping at one another," Brian replied, feigning innocence. "Should she have said something else?"

"No," Ivy replied, stepping in smoothly. "Everything is fine. We've all agreed to work together."

"I think that's a good idea," Brian said. "We're stronger together than we are apart."

"I totally agree," Max said, exchanging an amused look with Brian. "I want to help if I can, too."

"I think we're good on the help front," Jack said tersely. "We've got plenty of help."

"He's right," Brian said. "What we don't have is leads. We really need to identify the victim. That's going to be my main focus today."

"I'll help you," Jack said.

"Actually, I need you and Ivy to focus on those symbols," Brian replied, not missing a beat. "Don't you have a bunch of reference books out at your cottage, Ivy?"

Ivy was caught. She knew it. "Yes."

"I think you and Jack should go through those books today," Brian said, refusing to make eye contact. "It's probably going to be a long afternoon, but with both of you going at it, we have a better shot of identifying at least some of the symbols."

Jack cleared his throat, uncomfortable. "Don't you want me with you?"

"We only have two things to focus on," Brian replied. "I think we should split up and tackle them both at the same time. You and Ivy can handle the symbols. I'll see if I can identify the victim."

"But ... ."

"I think that's a great idea," Max said. "I'm positive I'll feel a lot better about Ivy being secluded in that house knowing that Jack is there with her. She won't be in danger that way."

Jack sighed, resigned, and then turned to Ivy. "Do you want to drive together or do you want me to follow you out there?"

"Oh, I drove her here," Max answered, exchanging a delighted look with Brian. "She's going to need a ride. Thank you so much for taking her."

"You're welcome," Jack said, staring at the empty spot in front of him. "Do you want to order breakfast first?"

Ivy didn't have much of an appetite, but she was desperate to delay being alone with Jack. "I'm starving."

"Me, too," Jack muttered, glaring at Brian.

"See, this is so much better than oatmeal, isn't it?"

Eleven

"Where should we start?" Jack asked, glancing around Ivy's small living room an hour later. "I don't see all these books that Brian was talking about."

Ivy arched a challenging eyebrow and gestured toward the small stack of books on the end of her coffee table. "This is not my book collection."

She started moving down the hallway, leaving Jack with no option but to follow. The first doorway they passed was open, and Jack couldn't stop himself from glancing inside. It was a large – especially for the size of the cottage – bathroom. The claw foot tub looked vintage, and the airy curtains gave the room a welcoming feeling.

Farther down was Ivy's bedroom, and Jack found himself openly staring at the queen-sized bed, Nicodemus stretched out on a patch-work comforter that was pulled tight at the corners of the four-poster. *Don't think about that,* he warned himself, forcing his attention back to Ivy as she led him to the last room in the hallway.

She smiled engagingly at him as she pushed the door open, and Jack couldn't help but suck in a breath when he realized what he was looking at. Three of the walls in the room were covered – floor to ceiling – with wooden bookshelves. He'd never seen this many books in one place outside of a library or store. The shelves were so high they had those ladders that slide along railings on each wall so Ivy could get things off the top shelves.

In the center of the room was a comfy looking couch and ottoman. That was the only other furniture present. Jack whistled, the sound low and impressed. "This is ... ."

"Nerdy. I know," Ivy said, sighing. "I love books. I can't explain it."

"I wasn't going to say nerdy," Jack said, chuckling. "It's ... beautiful."

Ivy was surprised. "Beautiful?"

"I can tell you spend a lot of time in this room," Jack said. "It's comfortable." He moved over to run his hands over the shelves. "These are handmade. Someone clearly went out of their way when they made these for you."

"Max made them," Ivy said.

"I kind of figured," Jack said, loving the feeling of the wood as he touched it. "You can tell he wanted something that would fit your personality."

"As in loud and overbearing?"

"As in ... amazing." Jack realized what he'd said, but it was too late to pull the words back into his mouth. Instead of acknowledging them, he pretended he hadn't uttered them. "Where should we start?"

Ivy pointed to the shelves on the far side of the room. "Those are the books that might be able to help us."

There had to be fifty leather-bound tomes there, all well taken care of and heavy looking. It was going to take them forever. Jack stepped up to the shelves, selecting one of the books and pulling it out to study. "So, this is a ... witch book?"

Ivy made a face, crossing her arms over her chest as she regarded him. "Do you want to talk about this before we start?"

Jack balked. "Talk about what?"

"Your attitude regarding witches."

"What makes you think I have an attitude about witches?"

"You have a funny way of saying the word," Ivy said. "For the record, I don't consider myself a witch. I consider myself a naturalist who leans toward certain … practices … and I'm a great proponent of the tenets of Wicca.

"I do not ride around on a broom, however," she continued. "I don't curse people. I don't make potions, although I do make lotion and soap. I don't cast spells. I don't try to eat small children. Oh, and last time I checked, I don't cackle when I laugh."

Jack couldn't stop himself from smiling. She was just so … serious. "Okay," he said. "I guess you're saying you're a nature lover. I think I can live with that."

"It's a little more than that," Ivy hedged, shifting from one foot to the other. "I am not a true Wiccan. I like a lot of their beliefs, and I happen to believe in karma. I'm more of a … mixture. I pick what I like and stick to it. In essence, I believe in being a good person and holding true to myself. I also believe in magic."

"That doesn't sound so bad."

"It's not," Ivy said. "There are some people in town, though, who don't understand that."

"Ava Moffett?"

Ivy smiled tightly. "She's part of the small group who believe I'm a Devil worshipper and am sacrificing babies during full moons."

Jack smirked. "I don't care what you believe, Ivy," he said. "You seem pretty … normal … to me. Well, other than your hair."

"I happen to like my hair."

"I didn't say I didn't like it. It just stands out."

Ivy sighed. "Do you want to ask me anything?"

"Yes."

Ivy was surprised. She'd expected him to insist on looking through the books instead of conversing. "Okay."

"Can someone pervert Wiccan beliefs to do evil?"

"People can pervert anything to do evil," Ivy said. "Wicca is very … peaceful, though. It's not about hurting anyone. That's what people don't seem to understand. Wicca is not Satanism. That's a common misconception."

"Do you get a lot of people trying to convert you? Brian told me this is a Christian town. I would guess they see you as something of a challenge."

"Most of the residents here are good people," Ivy replied. "They accept me for who I am. There are a few, though, who are ... dismissive ... of my beliefs and me. I've been dealing with it since I was a child. I'm used to it. I let it roll off of me."

Jack wasn't sure if he believed that, but he let it go. "You seem like a good person," he said. "I don't have a problem with your beliefs. You're a little ... touchy ... but you have a right to your feelings. I'm guessing people judge you by how you look, not who you are. I know how that is."

Ivy cocked her head to the side, considering. "People look at you and see a tough guy, don't they?"

Jack shrugged, hating the way her gaze made him feel.

"You're a lot more than people give you credit for," she said. "You're a ... deep thinker. I think you're a deep feeler, too."

"You're wrong there," Jack said. "I'm someone who likes to focus on my job. I do think about that, so I am a deep thinker. I don't really get close enough to people to feel anything, though. It's just not who I am."

Now Ivy was the doubtful one. The words were bold, but she had trouble believing them. "Well, that's too bad," she said. "Feeling things is the way of the world. You are who you are, though. We should probably get to work."

"We should," Jack agreed. "How about I start on one side and you start on the other?"

Ivy nodded. "Sure. We can meet in the middle."

FOUR HOURS LATER JACK'S BACK HURT AND HIS EYES WERE starting to cross. He'd flipped through so many books his fingers were starting to ache – and that was on top of the paper cuts.

He jumped when Ivy dropped a heavy book on the floor. "We need a break," she said.

"We still have at least half of these books to go through," Jack said.

"I know. We're starting to zone out, though. We need to refocus."

"What did you have in mind?"

Ivy smiled. "How about a walk?"

Jack stilled. "A walk?"

"I need some air," Ivy said. "I need to stretch my legs. This house is starting to feel small. Usually when I feel like this I go for a walk. I don't have to go if you're not in the mood, but I think it would do you some good, too."

Jack shrugged. "I could use a walk," he said. "A half hour away from this would probably let us recharge. Are we going to walk in the woods?"

"Is that okay with you?"

"That's fine," Jack said. "I like the woods. I didn't get a chance to really look around last night because your brother tossed me around like I was on the high school football team and I was trying to get the winning touchdown."

Ivy snickered. "I don't care what you say," she said. "I saw what you did. You could have seriously hurt him."

"I … it was a draw."

"Thank you for not hurting him," Ivy said, ignoring Jack's attempt at modesty. "He's a pain in the rear, but he's very important to me."

"I think you're important to him, too," Jack said. "Let's go for that walk. I'm kind of curious to look around. I love this parcel of land. It's very … peaceful."

"It is," Ivy said, getting to her feet. "Let's go."

IVY LED JACK OUT THROUGH THE FRONT DOOR, SETTING AN EASY pace as they loped into the woods. The trees were tall, and their wide boughs allowed for a lot of shade as the sun broke through in small glints.

Even though the silence was amiable, Jack was uncomfortable with it. This was his opportunity to learn more about Ivy, and he wasn't going to pass it up. "Did you spend a lot of time out here when you were a kid?"

"Max and I liked to play games," Ivy said. "We used to chuck pine cones at one another and pretend they were grenades, and we made a lot of forts."

"I heard you made a … what did Brian call it?"

Ivy glanced up at him, pursing her lips as she waited.

"A fairy ring," Jack said. "He said that all the kids in town went to church camp one summer and you stayed home and made a fairy ring. What is that?"

"Technically you can't make a fairy ring," Ivy clarified. "It has to be naturally occurring. That being said, I found a fairy ring and I cleaned up the area and made it a kind of ... hang out."

"Brian also said you still keep it up," Jack said. "Can I see it?"

The fairy ring – her special clearing in the forest – was Ivy's favorite place in the world. She rarely took people there, even Max. It was her private spot. Still, for some reason, she couldn't deny Jack. "Do you really want to see it?"

"I'm dying to see it," Jack said. "I have no idea what it is, and yet I haven't been able to get the idea out of my head since Brian mentioned it."

"Why?"

"I don't know," Jack replied honestly. "I keep picturing flowers ... and sunshine ... and magic."

"Do you believe in magic?"

"I don't know," Jack said, his voice soft. "I believe in evil. I've seen it. I would like to think there's something out there to counter it, even if I never get to see it with my own eyes."

"Okay then," Ivy said, giving in. "I'll show you some magic."

A wave of ... something ... ran down Jack's spine. He was already in the presence of magic, even if Ivy didn't know it. It was like the air was sparking around them – they just couldn't see it. "Let's go."

Jack followed Ivy, the duo occasionally chatting about specific trees and landmarks, but the trek was made mostly in silence. After about fifteen minutes, Ivy led Jack into a small clearing. It took Jack a few seconds to realize what he was looking at.

An old tree, one of those ancient husks that almost looks as if it has a face carved into it, rested on one side. In the middle, a large ring of mushrooms made a complete circle around a distinctive rock. It almost looked like a small altar. Between the chirping birds and far off trickle from a nearby creek, Jack was nearly convinced he'd crossed over into Heaven.

"This is … amazing."

"It's special," Ivy agreed, glancing around. "This is my favorite place on Earth."

"Do you come here often? Does Max come out here with you?"

"This is my … private place," Ivy said. "Max has been here. He always knew to come here to find me when I was late for dinner as a kid. He still let me have this place to myself."

Jack turned to her, his expression thoughtful. "If this is your private place, why did you bring me here?"

Ivy shrugged. "I just thought you might need a little magic."

The air between them zinged, and Jack unconsciously took a step toward her. His eyes were focused on her petal pink lips, and he couldn't force his mind to any other notion besides kissing her. He couldn't explain it, and he wasn't sure he could fight it.

Ivy appeared to be reading his mind because she didn't shy away when he moved toward her.

"What's happening?" Jack murmured, taking another step. She was only a foot away from him now.

"Magic," Ivy whispered, tilting her head up and widening her blue eyes.

Jack took the final step, his fingers grazing the side of her face, but instead of finding solid ground his ankle twisted as he stepped on a rock and he found himself falling. He just wasn't falling into her eyes – or upon her lips. He was tumbling toward the ground.

"Oh, crap!"

Twelve

All manly bravado fled Jack the second he hit the ground. His tailbone hurt and his wrist pinged with pain as he used it to absorb the bulk of his fall, but it was his pride that took the biggest beating.

Ivy's eyes were like saucers, the blue searching Jack's brown orbs for a hint that he was hurt. "Are you okay?"

"I'm fine," Jack said, grunting as he shifted.

"Are you sure?"

"I'm sure."

"That's good," Ivy said. Then she burst into hysterical gales of laughter, bending over at the waist and letting her whole body shake.

Jack scowled. "Are you laughing at me?"

"I can't help it," Ivy said, holding her hand to her midriff as she gasped for breath. "I just … it was like something out of a movie."

Jack didn't want to laugh, but Ivy was having such a good time it was contagious. Finally, he gave in and joined her. "Yes, it's very funny."

"You're such a big guy," Ivy said, collecting herself. "It was like you were falling in slow motion."

"I'm glad to serve as your entertainment." Jack leaned back on the ground, rolling slightly so he could gain his footing. He pushed off and climbed to his feet, rubbing his hands against his shirt and jeans to clean them once he was standing. "Are you done laughing now?"

Ivy pressed her lips together, uncertain. "I think so."

"I can wait until you're done."

"Are you sure?"

Jack waited, and when Ivy dissolved into giggles again, he couldn't help but join her as he rubbed the back of his neck wearily. "That's nice," he said.

"What is?" Ivy asked, wiping a mirthful tear from her eye.

"That's the first time I've seen you really laugh."

He was serious, and the tone of his voice caused Ivy to still. She hadn't forgotten where they'd been heading before Jack's tumble. "I'm sorry. Laughing at the misfortune of others isn't something I generally do."

"It's not like I lost a leg in a car accident or anything," Jack said. "I fell. Sometimes that's funny. I like seeing you laugh."

"Well, I'm done now," Ivy said, straightening. "Will you let me look you over quickly and make sure you're not hurt?"

"I'm fine," Jack said.

"Just humor me."

"I thought that's what I just did."

The smile Ivy flashed at Jack was utterly charming.

"Fine," he said. "Look me over."

Ivy circled him, her hands reaching out to touch his arm before she jerked them back. Her gaze was serious as she focused on the ground.

"What's wrong?" Jack asked, raising his hand to rub it against his chin.

"Don't do that!"

It was too late. Jack scratched his itch. "Don't do what?"

The expression on Ivy's face was no longer amused. Now it was sympathetic. "I ... um ... please try not to touch yourself. Anywhere."

Jack made a face. "Excuse me?"

Ivy pointed at the ground, gesturing toward the crushed plants with a rueful smile. "I know you can't tell now because you destroyed them, but ... ."

"Listen, I'm sorry I marred your fairy ring," Jack said, scratching his nose. "I didn't mean to wreck this for you."

Ivy pressed her lips together, horrified. "Jack, please stop touching your face."

"Why?"

"Those aren't just plants ... or weeds," Ivy said. "It's ... ironically ... Poison Ivy."

Jack's shoulders stiffened, and his face was a mask of worry and anger as he focused on Ivy. "What?"

"That's Poison Ivy. It spreads like wildfire, and your hands were in it."

"You're saying I'm infected with Poison Ivy?"

Ivy moved closer to him, focusing on his neck. "You've already spread it to your neck, and I'm going to guess to your nose. Since you were rolling around down there, I'm a little worried it's on your back, too."

"What should I do? Do I need to go to the hospital?" Jack was a city boy. He had no idea how to deal with nature problems. Despite himself, he was starting to panic. A gangbanger with a sawed-off shotgun he could handle. This, though, was something that might just render him catatonic.

"I have a cream back at the cottage," Ivy said, drawing his attention back to her. "It will stop the spread and ease the itching. I just need you to really try to keep your hands away from your face."

"Okay," Jack said. "Let's go. Now that I know what this is, all I want to do is scratch my face."

"Don't scratch anything else either," Ivy warned, somber.

"Like what?"

"Anything ... down there," Ivy said, pointing toward the crotch of his jeans.

"Why would I do that?"

"I have no idea," Ivy said. "I just know Max did it when he was a teenager – he was out in the woods with Becky Saunders and they were rolling around – and he said nothing ever hurt that badly in his entire life. He's still haunted by it. He's broken a couple of bones and dislocated his shoulder, so I take him at his word."

"I'm not an animal," Jack said. "I have no intention of scratching anything. You can rest assured that I won't be doing … that."

"Okay," Ivy said, giving him a wide berth as she circled back around and headed toward the cabin. "Keep close … but try not to touch me."

"I think I can control myself."

"I'm sure you can."

Jack was glad she had faith, because now that she had told him what not to scratch that was all he could think about scratching. "I have the worst luck ever," he grumbled.

"Did you say something?"

"Pick up your pace. I'm suffering here."

BY THE TIME THEY GOT BACK TO THE COTTAGE JACK WAS A mess. He kept imagining an army of angry red bumps all over his face. Well, he'd been looking for something to keep the women of Shadow Lake at bay – this just wasn't what he had in mind.

"Sit down on the kitchen table," Ivy instructed. "The cream is in the bathroom. I'll be back in one minute. Take your shirt off."

Jack balked. "Why?"

"Honey, it's on your neck. I saw it when we came into the house. That means it's on your back. It spreads. I need to put the cream anywhere you've been exposed."

Jack scowled. "I can put it on my own back."

"Don't be such a baby," Ivy said, moving toward the hallway. "The sooner I can get this cream on you the better."

Jack watched her go, dread washing over him. He couldn't take his shirt off. He wouldn't. There had to be another way. He couldn't let her … see.

When Ivy returned to the kitchen she had a bottle of lotion in her hand and a frown on her face. "I told you to take your shirt off."

"I feel fine on my back," Jack lied. "Just handle my hands and face. I'll be okay."

"I don't know what this modesty thing is, but I don't like it," Ivy said. "Poison Ivy can be serious. Now, lift your arms. I've seen plenty of men without their shirts on before. I promise not to jump you if that's what you're worried about. I'm not a teenage girl ... and you're not that hot."

Jack made a face. "I ... no."

"That did it," Ivy snapped. "I'm not joking around here. I don't know what you're embarrassed about, but trust me, I've seen it all. Now, lift your arms over your head right now!"

Jack was so surprised by her vehemence he had no choice. He reluctantly lifted his arms, resigned, and Ivy's hands were on the bottom hem of the shirt and whipping it over his head before he could think of a reason to stop her.

Ivy dropped the shirt on the table next to him, her gaze focused on his neck. She hadn't seen his deep, dark secret yet. It was only a matter of time, though. Jack fixed his eyes on the floor. He didn't want to see the revulsion on her face when she finally worked her way around and saw ... everything.

Instead of looking at his front, though, Ivy tipped the bottle of lotion and rubbed the cool substance onto the fiery spot on his back. She rubbed it in partially and then left it sitting on top of the rash. "It needs to soak in."

"Okay," Jack mumbled.

Ivy moved to his front, practically growling when she saw his muscled arms and chiseled chest. His eight-pack abs were moving in and out as he sucked in an uneasy breath, and she couldn't understand what he was so worked up about. And then she saw it.

On the left side of his chest, below his shoulder and above his heart, there were two angry scars. They were both round and raised, and Ivy knew what they were without being told. They were bullet wounds. He'd been shot. Twice. The location would seem to indicate he'd been lucky to survive.

Without realizing what she was doing, Ivy's fingertips traveled to the scars, tracing them lightly. Jack refused to meet her questioning eyes, so she leaned in and brushed her lips against his ear. "It's okay," she whispered. "You don't have to tell me. You don't have to be ashamed."

Jack involuntary shuddered at her words – and her touch – and he finally found the courage to lift his head. Her face was serious, but she didn't look disgusted or frightened. "You don't want to know?"

"No," Ivy said. "You don't want to tell me. If you ever do, I'll want to know. It's not my business. You can wait until you're ready."

"What makes you think I'll ever be ready?"

Ivy shrugged and poured more of the lotion into her hand, rubbing it over an angry spot of skin on his neck and causing him to almost cry out in relief when the soothing salve wiped away the torturous itchiness. "I don't know if you'll ever be ready," Ivy said. "I just know that you're not ready now. I would never try to force you into telling me. That's not who I am."

"I … this isn't something I want people talking about."

"Do you think I would spread your secret all over town?"

"No," Jack said, shaking his head as he realized she wouldn't be capable of something like that. "I moved here to put all of … this … behind me."

"I understand," Ivy said, shifting her hands to the spot under his chin. "Lift up here, please."

Jack did as instructed. He no longer had any place to look but Ivy's eyes. It was like being lost at sea, and she was the only boat within swimming distance. "I've never met anyone like you."

"What do you mean?"

"You're just so comfortable in your own skin," he said. "You know who you are, and you're not afraid to be the person you were born to be. You don't try to conform to what other people want. You're just you."

"That's the way I was raised," Ivy said. "I don't see why you're surprised. You're the same way."

"I'm not sure I am," Jack said, his eyes moving to her plump lips. "I'm afraid to be the person I am. I'm afraid I've turned myself into a … monster."

Ivy chuckled hollowly. "A monster? You're not a monster. You're conflicted, and you're trying to find even footing, but you're as far from a monster as anyone can get."

"What makes you say that?"

"I can feel your soul," Ivy said softly. "It's … beautiful."

Their lips were close. Too close. Jack couldn't fight the urge. Not again. He lifted his chin slightly and their lips met before he could think better about what he was doing. The kiss was light at the start, but as they both leaned in to deepen it, things turned needy.

Jack found he was lifting his hands to run through her hair and pull her closer – but the reality of the Poison Ivy caught up with him before he could give in to his baser instincts. He wouldn't hurt her … not for anything in this world.

They pulled apart at the same time, both of them gasping for air.

Ivy's hand flew up to her mouth, her eyes wide. "I'm so sorry."

"For what?" Jack asked, struggling to clear the lovesick cobwebs from his mind. "I … I'm the one who did it. I'm the one who is sorry."

"I think we both did it," Ivy said, making a face. "I just … I wasn't expecting it. I didn't mean to … I'm not sure we should … I just … ."

Jack couldn't stop himself from laughing, breaking the spell but chasing the pall from the room. "Relax, Ivy. We didn't do anything wrong. We didn't do anything we can't take back. It was just an … impulse."

Ivy nodded, relieved. "Just an impulse."

"Right," he said, his heartbeat slowly returning to normal. "People have impulses all of the time. It doesn't necessarily mean anything. It was just a charged moment."

"Right." Ivy blew an extended breath out, blowing her hair away from her forehead. "It was just a stupid impulse. Here … don't move … I'm not done with your face yet. Once I'm done, you should be good to go."

"That's good," Jack said, internally sighing. That was the one thing he desperately needed to do now: go. If he stayed, he knew darned well that impulses would get the better of them again, and he wasn't sure he would have the strength to stop himself a second time.

The truth was, he wasn't sure he wanted to stop himself – and that was a frightening thought.

Thirteen

"You look like you've seen better days," Brian said, studying Jack the next morning as the younger detective sat at his desk. "What's on your neck?"

"Poison Ivy."

"Is that a euphemism for something you and Ivy did yesterday afternoon?" Brian asked, intrigued.

"No, it's Poison Ivy," Jack said. "I fell in it yesterday. It's better than it was, but I still have to rub lotion all over my body to keep myself from shredding my own skin because it itches so badly."

Brian had to work hard to swallow his laugh. "How did you fall in Poison Ivy while you were supposed to be looking through books?"

"We took a break to get some air," Jack replied, indignant. "Thanks for saddling me with fifty million witch books, by the way."

"You're welcome," Brian replied, nonplussed. "I wasn't saddling you with the books, though."

"Yeah, I figured that out," Jack said. "Don't think I don't know what you and Max were trying to do yesterday."

"I'm guessing it didn't work."

There was no way Jack was going to let on just how close Brian and Max had gotten to achieving their goal. "No, it didn't," he said.

"We went for a walk because we needed some fresh air and I fell into … this."

"What did Ivy do?"

"She laughed."

Brian snickered. "Did she at least help you after the fact?"

"Where do you think I got the lotion?"

"I really am sorry," Brian said. "I've had Poison Ivy before. It can be miserable. The lotion should have you back to full capacity by tomorrow, though. Just be sure you don't scratch anything in the … um … southern hemisphere."

Jack made a face. "Ivy warned me about that," he said. "Is that really a thing? She said it happened to Max once."

"It's a thing," Brian said. "I got Poison Ivy when I was younger while camping, and I had to go to the bathroom before I realized what was going on and … well … let me just say, there is no pain worse than that. I think it's even worse than childbirth, although I have no way of comparing the two."

Jack rolled his eyes. "You're really enjoying this, aren't you?"

"I'm sorry you're miserable," Brian said. "You do seem somehow … lighter, though. I think spending the afternoon with Ivy did you some good. She has a way of bringing people out of their shells."

"I don't have a shell."

"Son, you're practically a turtle," Brian said. "Don't worry, though. You'll be okay. You're just adjusting. It will take a little time. Did you and Ivy find anything in the books?"

"No," Jack said, cracking his neck. "I couldn't focus on the books after the Poison Ivy incident, so I just left. I think she was going to continue looking, but she said she would call if she found something. I'm guessing she didn't call."

"No," Brian said, shaking his head. "For now it appears the symbols are a dead end. While you were rolling around in the woods with Ivy Morgan, though, I did manage to get somewhere."

"You'd better stop saying things like that," Jack said, shooting Brian a look. "You have a big mouth, and if people start talking about us … doing things … I'm going to be ticked."

"Why? Are you embarrassed to be seen with Ivy?"

"Of course not," Jack said. "I just don't want people thinking I'm open for offers. That's not why I moved here. That's not what I want."

"You've told me," Brian said. "I'm not trying to force anything on you."

"You're trying to force Ivy Morgan on me," Jack countered. "Don't bother denying it. I know exactly what you and her brother were doing yesterday. I'm not stupid."

"Do you want to know what I think?"

"Not particularly."

"I think you're worried because you want Ivy to be forced on you," Brian said. "I think from the moment you laid eyes on her she's about the only thing you've been able to think about."

"Are you saying I'm not doing my job?" Jack asked, his eyes narrowed.

"Absolutely not," Brian said. "You seem like a dedicated officer. Never think that's what I'm getting at. I just think you're being … tugged … in a certain direction, and that direction just happens to be on the same side of town where Ivy lives."

"I think you're making things up in your own mind," Jack shot back.

"Well … I guess we'll have to agree to disagree," Brian said. "Not that I don't want to continue this discussion, but I did manage to get somewhere yesterday."

Jack leaned forward, interested. "Did you identify our victim?"

"I did," Brian said. "It took some work, but I found her." Brian reached inside the file on his desk and removed a photograph, the blonde teenager in it smiling brightly as Jack focused on her face. "Meet Mona Wheeler."

"What do we know about her?" Jack asked, his heart rolling painfully as he studied the young woman, worry over his own ailments quickly fleeing.

"Well, she was originally from Bellaire," Brian said. "She grew up there, and she graduated from the high school last spring."

"Why didn't her parents report her missing?"

"They didn't know she was missing," Brian said. "They're on their way in here now, though, so be careful what you say. The girl was a student at Central Michigan University, and she was just finishing up her freshman year. They were expecting her to move home for the summer this weekend. I talked to them over the phone, and they were … devastated. They honestly didn't appear to know that she was even missing."

"How did she end up here?"

"That's one of the things we need to find out."

"I DON'T understand. She was supposed to be in Mount Pleasant. How did she end up in Shadow Lake?"

Under normal circumstances, Evan Wheeler looked like he was a bull of a man. His shoulders were broad, his chest barreled. The loss of his daughter had crippled him, though. His skin – which was probably tan and robust on a normal day – was sallow. His eyes were red and puffy from hours of crying, and his hands were shaking.

His wife, Cathy, was even worse. She hadn't uttered a word since entering the police station. Instead, she'd sat in the chair, covered her mouth with her hand, and proceeded to rock herself. She was obviously in shock.

"We were hoping you would know why she was over here," Brian said.

"I have no idea," Evan said. "She was at school. She had finals this week. We expected her to come home on Saturday. I mean tomorrow. Tomorrow is Saturday, right?"

Brian nodded. "Sir … ."

"How did she die?" Evan asked, cutting Brian off. "Where did you find her?"

"She was found in a ditch on the other side of town," Brian said carefully. "She was … stabbed multiple times."

Cathy made a mewling sound in the back of her throat. Evan leaned over and rested his arm on her shoulders. It was supposed to be soothing, but Evan couldn't soothe himself, so helping his wife was out of the question.

"Was she raped?" Evan asked, forcing his face to remain solid.

"There were signs of sexual activity," Brian said. "We can't be sure if it was rape until we're further into the investigation."

"Well, my daughter was a good girl," Evan said. "If she had sex, she was forced to do it. She didn't do ... that."

"Are you sure?" Brian asked.

"Of course I'm sure," Evan snapped. "She's my daughter."

Jack leaned forward, keeping his voice low and even. "Sir, there is absolutely no offense intended here. It's just ... teenage girls aren't known for talking to their fathers about sex. I'm not insinuating you're wrong. We just have to be sure."

"She was a good girl," Evan said, his voice firm.

Jack glanced at Cathy. "Mrs. Wheeler, can you confirm that?"

Jack wasn't surprised when Cathy started shaking her head. Evan blanched. "What?"

"She didn't want you to know," Cathy said. "I didn't blame her. I knew you wouldn't take it well. I took her to get birth control pills before she left for the school year."

"How could you?"

"I didn't want us to be grandparents at an early age," Cathy said. "I wanted her to be as safe as she could be."

"Well, good news," Evan snapped. "Now we're never going to be grandparents."

Cathy dissolved into tears again.

"Sir, I know you're upset," Jack said. "I don't think ... ."

"Don't tell me how to react," Evan said. "I'm just ... that was my baby."

"I understand," Jack said. "I'm very sorry for your loss."

"We both are," Brian said. "We do have some questions, though."

"I know," Evan said, rubbing the heel of his hand against his eye. "Go ahead. I know you have a job to do."

"When was the last time you saw your daughter, Mr. Wheeler?"

"Over Easter," Evan said. "She came home for the holiday and then went back to school in the afternoon on Easter Sunday."

"Was it normal to go so long without seeing her?"

"She was a college student," Evan said, shrugging helplessly. "She was caught between being a kid and being an adult. She was trying to cement her independence."

"What do you mean by that?"

"She was ... I don't know ... different," Evan said. "She was still my daughter, don't get me wrong. She wasn't the same kid we raised, though. I was hoping a summer at home would get her back to where she was."

"We need more details," Jack prodded.

"She was running with a bad crowd," Evan said.

"Drugs?"

"No," Evan said, shaking his head. "That's one thing I'm sure about. There weren't any drugs." He shot a look in Cathy's direction for confirmation. "Right?"

"I wouldn't have sat back and let her take drugs without telling you," Cathy said, frustrated. "Drugs are not the same thing as birth control."

"I don't want to talk about this here," Evan said, crossing his arms over his chest.

"Fine," Cathy said. "Just don't ... look at me like that. It's not my fault she's dead."

"I didn't say it was."

"Then stop acting like it."

This was going to spiral out of control if Jack couldn't get it under control. He cleared his throat. "When you said she was hanging around with a bad crowd, what did you mean?"

"You expect a certain level of ... change ... in your child when they go away to college," Evan said. "I expected some partying. I expected some trouble adjusting to harder classes. I expected new political interests. What Mona was doing was ... different."

Jack waited.

"She started talking about ... weird things," Evan said. "She got really into religion, only it wasn't a normal religion."

"What kind of religion?"

"It was weird," Evan said. "She kept talking about people being passengers. She stopped believing in Jesus all of a sudden, and she started talking about being vessels for an alien passenger on this

Earth until she passed on to some other form of … higher living. These are her words, mind you. I don't believe in any of that nonsense."

"She never said she believed she was a passenger," Cathy said. "She was just … interested … in this new religion. She couldn't stop talking about it."

"It was crazy," Evan said.

"When did you first notice a change in her demeanor?"

"I guess it was around Christmas," Evan said, rubbing the back of his neck. "The first time I really noticed it was when we were getting ready for Mass on Christmas Eve and she told us she wasn't going. She said she wasn't a Christian and she couldn't go into the church because it would be blasphemous."

"What did you do?"

"I yelled at her," Evan admitted. "I thought she was just being difficult to be difficult. She is … she was … still a teenager. They say and do things just to get a rise out of you sometimes.

"Eventually I just let it go," he continued. "I figured giving her what she wanted – which I was sure was an argument – was a bad idea. I guess I should have dug my feet in then."

"You can't second guess yourself, sir," Jack said. "You can't bring her back, and you'll just drive yourself crazy if you spend all of your time trying to figure out how you would go back and change things."

"I know," Evan said. "When she came home for Easter she was a completely different person. She was dressing in these weird ankle-length skirts, and she insisted on making sure her arms were completely covered. She kept going on and on about modesty being key."

"Did you try to talk to her?"

"We did," Evan said. "She wouldn't listen, though. Eventually, we agreed to let her go back to school. We were going to tackle it as a team when she got back under our roof. We figured three months with us would get her back on the right path."

Jack fought the pinch in his heart. "Can you remember your daughter mentioning any names of the people she was hanging out with?"

"Just one," Evan said. "In fact, she said his name so many times I thought he might be paying her for the publicity."

"Who?"

"Chad Hamilton."

Brian made a face, but Jack opted to ignore it for the time being. Whatever the older detective was thinking it wasn't something he wanted to share with the Wheelers.

"Can you think of anything else that might be of importance to us going forward?"

Evan shook his head. "No. I just want to go home. I want to take my daughter home. Can I do that now?"

Jack nodded. "I really am sorry for your loss, sir. The only thing I can promise is that I won't quit until I find out who did this to her."

"You do that," Evan said. "Then, when you find him, call me. I'll take care of the justice."

Fourteen

"What do you think?"

After showing the Wheelers out, and directing them toward the funeral parlor where Mona's body was being held, Jack and Brian found themselves back in their office with more answers and another mountain of questions to tackle.

"I think it sounds like Mona Wheeler was involved with a cult," Brian said.

Jack arched an eyebrow. "A cult?"

"What did it sound like to you?"

"It sounded like a cult," Jack conceded. "I've just never had the misfortune of actually running into one."

"You're from the city," Brian said. "Are you saying they don't have cults in the city?"

"I'm sure they do," Jack replied, nonplussed. "I've just never interacted with one. Do you want to tell me who this Chad Hamilton guy is?"

Brian narrowed his eyes. "What do you mean?"

"I know you recognized the name," Jack said. "Don't bother denying it. I saw the look on your face when the father brought him up. What do you know about him?"

Brian sighed, leaning back in his desk chair and staring up at the ceiling. "I do know Chad Hamilton."

"Tell me about him."

"He was the same age as my youngest son, Sean," Brian said.

"But ... the Wheelers made it sound like this Chad was a student along with their daughter," Jack argued.

"I know. That's one of the things that worries me."

"Go back to telling me about Chad."

"He was a normal kid when he was younger," Brian said. "In fact, he was better than a normal kid. He didn't join any cliques, and he wasn't one to hang around with the bullying group like Ava and Maisie."

"So, what happened?"

"I have no idea," Brian said. "Chad was one heck of an athlete. I can tell you that. He was the captain of the football team, and the basketball team, and the baseball team ... oh, and he bowled in his father's league on the weekends."

"You've got to be kidding me."

"No, he was the all-around American teenager," Brian said. "He got good grades. He was a virtual ... golden boy."

"How well did you know him?"

"Pretty well," Brian said. "He and Sean were fairly tight. They were on a couple teams together. Chad was always happy to help, and we paid him during planting and harvesting season every year. He was a good worker."

"This doesn't sound like a problem kid ... err ... adult," Jack said.

"Things kind of ... shifted ... senior year," Brian explained. "Chad had his pick of schools. The University of Michigan offered him a football scholarship, and Michigan State University offered him a base-ball scholarship.

"My understanding was that he was actually leaning toward the baseball scholarship," he continued. "His parents figured his career would be longer and he'd be less likely to be hurt if he made it to the professional level."

"They're both good schools," Jack said. "Which one did he go to?"

"Neither. On the first play of the first home football game of his senior year he was blindsided during a hit," Brian said. "He tore his ACL, and he was done for the season."

"That happens to athletes."

"It does, and while Chad was disappointed about missing out on his final football season, he had rehab to get through and they figured he'd be fine by the time baseball season rolled around," Brian said. "The problem is, by the time baseball season came, Chad was still struggling. He never healed right, and the doctors said they couldn't go in and fix the damage."

"Oh, that's too bad," Jack said. "His athletic career was over before it started."

"Chad didn't take it well," Brian said. "He started raising hell all over town. There was a lot of drinking … and partying … and there were rumors about girls, although I'm not sure how true those were because he had a serious girlfriend.

"The real blow came when his scholarship was withdrawn," Brian said. "His parents didn't have the money to send him to Michigan State without financial help, and the idea of having to go to community college for two years pretty much crushed the life right out of that boy."

"What happened?"

"Nothing at first," Brian said. "When the fall hit, all of Chad's classmates moved on. Some of them went to college. Some of them got married. The rest got jobs. The only one stuck in place was Chad."

"How did he take it?"

"He kept hanging around the high school kids," Brian said. "The kids who were juniors when he was a senior became his new best friends. I didn't think much about it at the time. I figured he was just lonely and he didn't know what else to do. They were close to the same age, after all.

"The problem is, he kept doing it year after year," he continued. "Five years after he graduated from high school he was still hanging out with the teenagers at the local party spots. Now he was old enough to buy, though, and he was really popular."

"Let me guess, he thought he was a hero to these kids when he was really just a way for them to get their hands on alcohol," Jack supplied.

"Pretty much," Brian said. "Each year that passed Chad got more and more bitter. Then, four years ago, something else happened."

"You like to be dramatic when you're telling a story, don't you?"

Brian rolled his eyes. "Three seniors from the 2012 graduating class held up the bank at gunpoint. They stole two grand, and they shot a security guard in the process. He survived, and we caught the kids with the money two hours later."

"Was Chad with them?"

"No."

"What does he have to do with the story?"

"Those kids swore up and down Chad somehow convinced them to rob that bank," Brian said. "They said they didn't want to, but Chad magically made them do it against their will."

"You didn't believe them, did you?"

"Of course not," Brian replied. "Even if he did tell them to rob the bank they were still old enough to know their actions were wrong. The case went to trial, and the kids screamed to the heavens that it was all Chad's fault, but in the end they were convicted and Chad was a free man."

"What happened next?"

"Well, I figured the next fall would be the same," Brian said. "I thought Chad would show up at the party spot and start hanging out with the kids. To my surprise, he wasn't there, though. He was gone."

"Where did he go?"

"I didn't hear a thing about him for almost two years," Brian said. "Then ... well ... I started hearing whispers about a group of people at a commune up by Central Lake."

"A commune?"

"It's kind of like a hippie community," Brian explained. "They live off the grid. They build their own houses – more like boxy warehouses really – and they plant their own crops. They don't use cell phones, and they're against technology. There are no computers or power lines. It's completely self-sufficient."

"And that's where Chad lives?"

"Chad is in charge," Brian said.

"How do you know that?"

"Well, Frank Wells came to see me about a year ago," Brian said. "His daughter, Shelly, went missing and he was convinced she was at that commune. She was seventeen when she took off, so she was technically still a minor. He was so adamant that I decided to go up there."

"What happened?" Jack was enthralled with the story.

"When I first got up there, I was shocked," Brian admitted. "I expected six people sitting around a fire passing a peace pipe."

Jack smirked. "Did you think they were growing more than vegetables?"

"It's always been a suspicion of mine, although I could never prove it," Brian said. "When I got up there, though, there were at least twenty people. I think there were probably more. I had this feeling like I was being watched. I never saw them, though, so I can't say for certain.

"Anyway, I walked up a hill and there was Chad," he continued. "I hadn't seen the boy in a few years, so his appearance was … jarring. He'd let his hair grow long, and he had one of those long beards. He was walking around in robes – strutting really. It was almost as if he thought he was Jesus Christ himself.

"He was standing in the middle of everyone preaching," Brian said. "I didn't really listen to what he was saying. It was utter nonsense. I do remember a little something about passengers, though. For the life of me I don't remember what the gist of it was."

"Did he recognize you? Was he happy to see you?"

"He started preaching that I was invading their space," Brian said. "He recognized me for sure. He also preached about me being the enemy."

"Did you find Shelly?"

"She was there. She was pregnant."

Jack furrowed his brow. "Who was the father?"

"She wouldn't say," Brian said. "In fact, she refused to say anything. Every question I asked she ignored. Every time I tried to get her to look at me she looked the other way. Finally, I had no choice but to take her into custody. I took her back to her father."

"What happened when she gave birth?"

"I have no idea," Brian said. "The day Shelly turned eighteen she took off again. She was about eight months pregnant at the time. She returned to the commune, and I don't believe she's talked to her parents since. I guess she's still up there."

"What do you think is going on?" Jack asked.

"I think Chad might be one of those weird polygamist types who is trying to repopulate the world," Brian said. "I know that sounds ... odd ... but that's the feeling I got. There were some men up at the commune, but the vast majority of bodies up there were of the female persuasion."

"Do you think Chad has started recruiting at colleges?"

"He might not have recruited Mona at college," Brian said. "She's from the next town over. Chad might have run into her somewhere else."

"I guess we're going up to see Chad then," Jack said. "Should we leave now?"

"Well ... there's something else you should probably know," Brian said.

"What?"

"I told you Chad had a serious girlfriend when he was in high school," Brian said. "She was the one person who tried to stand by him ... even when his behavior started to really fall apart."

"Is she up at the commune?"

"No, she dumped him when he refused to stop hanging around high school kids and try to build a future for himself," Brian said. "She put up with as much as she could and then she walked away."

"Do you want to talk to her about Chad before we go up?"

"That's the last thing I want to do," Brian said. "I think it's necessary, though."

Jack rocked to his feet. "Okay. Where is she? I'll go and talk to her if you're uncomfortable with the situation."

"Oh, that's good," Brian said, forcing a smile onto his face. "I think that's a great idea."

Jack furrowed his brow, confused. "Who is she."

"Her name is Ivy Morgan."

Jack's heart sank. "You've got to be kidding me."

"I wish I was."

"Well … crap."

"Have fun with your talk," Brian said, turning his attention to his desk.

"Wait, you expect me to do this myself? I thought … ."

"You just offered," Brian said.

"That was before I knew it was Ivy."

"Well, it's too late now," Brian said. "Have fun."

Jack growled, annoyed. "You set me up."

"That's a horrible thing to say about your new partner."

"I … ."

"You're right, though," Brian said. "You should get going now so you don't interrupt her dinner hour. I believe her parents are coming home today. You're going to want to get to her before they do."

"Why? What's wrong with them?"

"There's nothing wrong with them," Brian said. "They're just … free spirited."

"Is that code for something?"

"I guess you'll have to find that out on your own."

Jack couldn't be sure, but as he trudged toward the door, he was almost positive he could hear Brian chuckling. He just knew things were about to get worse, if that was even possible.

Fifteen

"There she is! There's my favorite child."

Michael Morgan bowed his six-foot frame and engulfed Ivy in a bear hug. His face, though more lined than she remembered when he left for Florida in the fall, was one of the most welcome sights Ivy had ever seen. "Daddy!"

"How is *she* your favorite child?" Max asked from behind his father, fixing Ivy with a dark look. "I'm the one who picked you up from the airport. I'm the one who carried all of your luggage into your house. I'm also the one who drove you over here because you were – and I quote – 'too tired to drive.' I'm your favorite child."

"You're one of them," Michael said, pinching Max's cheek affectionately. "I've already seen you, though. This is my first glimpse of my Ivy."

Max rolled his eyes and pushed his way into Ivy's cottage. "Whatever. I just think you don't appreciate me."

"We appreciate you," Luna Morgan said, using her diminutive hip to move her husband away so she could draw Ivy to her. "We appreciate you both. How is my favorite girl?"

"I'm good," Ivy said, beaming at her mother. "How are you? How was Florida?"

Since her parents had started spending winters in a balmier climate two years before, Ivy was of two minds: She missed them terribly while they were gone, but it was also a relief not to worry about them during Michigan's brutal winters. It was a trade-off, but one she was happy to make to keep them safe.

"It's too warm for me this time of year," Luna said, taking a seat on Ivy's couch and reaching over so she could snag Nicodemus. "We're thinking of cutting our trip short by a month next year. It's nice to be out of the snow, but I do love Michigan springs."

"I love Michigan springs, summers, and falls," Ivy said. "I could do without the winters, but it's just three months. It gives me time to catch up on my reading."

"How is the nursery?" Michael asked, sitting next to his wife and reaching over so he could stroke the cat. "I'll be ready to start work on Monday."

Michael and Luna were silent partners in both Max and Ivy's respective businesses. They essentially came and went as they pleased, but Michael was known to love planting season because he liked to impart his botanical wisdom on anyone who listened.

"Are you sure you don't want a few more days to get settled?" Ivy asked.

"I've been off for almost six months," Michael replied. "I'm ready for work. I think your mother and I have just about hit our bonding quota for the year."

Ivy smirked. Her parents liked to give each other a hard time but, after thirty-two years together, they were still desperately in love. "Knock yourself out," Ivy said.

"What's that smell?" Luna asked, wrinkling her nose. "Is that your famous vegetarian lasagna?"

"It is," Ivy said, her eyes sparkling. "I wasn't expecting you for another half hour, though. You're going to have to tough it out until dinner is ready."

"I think we can survive," Michael said. "It will give us a chance to catch up. What's new with you?"

Ivy shrugged, her mind momentarily flashing to Jack's eyes … and abs … and arms … and smile … . "What did you ask?"

Max rolled his eyes and smirked, but wisely kept his mouth shut.

"He asked what was new in your life," Luna supplied. "Does that smile on your face have something to do with your new boyfriend?"

Ivy balked. "What boyfriend?"

"Oh, don't play coy," Luna said. "Max told us about your new boyfriend. Is he really a police officer?"

Ivy's blue eyes narrowed as she scowled at her brother. "Max told you about my new boyfriend? Really?"

Max suddenly found something of interest to study on the wall behind Ivy's head. "I think they're exaggerating."

"You said she was hot for him," Michael said, guileless. "Those were the first words out of your mouth when we got off the airplane."

"He's making that up," Max said, laughing nervously.

"No, I'm not," Michael said. "You said that Ivy is drooling over the new cop and the new cop is drooling right back over her. I'm getting older. I'm not losing my hearing."

"I'm going to kill you," Ivy snapped, extending a finger in Max's direction. "You are just … ."

"Wait … are you saying he's not your boyfriend?" Luna asked, disappointed.

"He's not my boyfriend," Ivy said. "He's … a nice man who is investigating the death of a young woman who was found in my yard. Did Max tell you that, too?"

"He did," Luna acknowledged. "I'm sorry that happened to you. It must have been jarring."

"It wasn't my favorite part of the week," Ivy said dryly.

"Well, I'm sure it will be solved soon," Luna said. "Tell me about Jack."

Ivy scorched Max with a look. "You told her his name?"

"It just came up in conversation," Max said. "It was an honest mistake."

"I'm going to kill you."

"That can wait," Michael said. "Tell us about this Jack. Max says he's tall and strong. I'm not sure how he knows he's strong, but it was a nice detail."

"Well, Jack was walking through the woods the other night

because he was trying to make sure that the woman's body wasn't dragged through there before being dumped and Max tackled him because he thought he was a killer," Ivy said, relishing the fact that she could now turn the conversation back around on her brother.

"It's nice that he was looking out for you," Michael said, nonplussed.

"Jack kicked his butt."

Max made a face. "He didn't kick my butt. He took me by surprise. I was just about to make my move."

"I'm sure you were, son," Michael said, grinning. "What's this man's relationship status?"

Ivy shifted in her chair. "What?"

"Is he married?"

"I have no idea."

"You shouldn't be dating him if he's married," Michael said.

"I am not dating him," Ivy snapped. "We've worked together on the case – but only because there were some symbols carved into the girl's skin and Jack thinks they're pagan. That is the limit to our involvement."

Michael shifted his attention back to Max. "You said they were dating."

"Oh, they're going to be," Max said. "They're terrified to touch each other and you can pretty much feel the sexual tension rolling off of them when they're in the same room."

"That sounds exciting," Luna said, leaning forward. "What does he look like?"

"We are not dating," Ivy said. "We're not going to date. I'm sure he's a very nice man for someone – and I don't believe he's married, so don't worry about that. We're not going to date, though. We're acquaintances. I don't care what lies Max filled your heads with during the drive over here. We're not together … and we're not going to be together."

Max shifted his attention to the front window of the cottage, smirking when something caught his attention outside. "Hey, Ivy?"

"What?"

"Your ... acquaintance ... is here," Max said. "He's heading toward the front door."

Luna clapped her hands together, thrilled. "This is so exciting!"

Ivy could think of another word to describe it. She just couldn't say it in front of her parents.

JACK RAISED HIS HAND TO KNOCK ON THE DOOR, WONDERING one more time if he was missing a way to get out of this conversation. He didn't get a chance to come up with an excuse to leave because the door popped open, revealing Ivy's expectant face.

"Um ... hi."

"Hi," Ivy said, hopping from one foot to the next. "I ... um ... ."

"About last night ... ."

"You don't have to say a thing about it," Ivy said, shaking her head vehemently. "Don't say one word."

"I think I should," Jack said. "I ... ."

Ivy reached over and slapped her hand over Jack's mouth, taking him by surprise. "Not one word."

He widened his eyes, surprised. She never did things like a normal person. He had a feeling that was one of the reasons he couldn't get her out of his mind. Her lips, which were currently pressed together and pouty, were another reason. "Okay," Jack said, taking a step back. Her touch was electric, and he needed a little space if his mind was going to work. "You didn't have to do that."

"I think I did," Ivy hissed. "I ... ."

The door opened wider, and the man standing behind Ivy took Jack by surprise. "I'm sorry. I didn't realize you had guests. I can ... come back later."

"That might be better," Ivy said, relieved.

"That won't be necessary," the man said. "I'm Michael Morgan, Ivy's father. We've heard a lot about you. Why don't you come in?"

Jack froze. "You've heard a lot about me?" He glanced at Ivy.

"Don't look at me," Ivy said, crossing her arms over her chest and scowling. "You can blame Max for that."

Jack fought the mad urge to laugh. "I see. Um … well … I don't want to interrupt. I can come back later."

"Oh, no, we can't have that," Michael said, grabbing Jack's arm and tugging him inside of the house. "You're already here. You're not interrupting anything. We're all caught up. Now we want to meet you."

Jack's gaze connected with Ivy's flat features. "Are you sure?"

"Oh, he's never going to let you go now," Ivy said. "You either need to beat him up – like you did Max – or suck it up and come on in."

"Is beating him up an option?"

"It's up to you," Ivy said. "I'm fine either way you want to go."

Jack sighed, resigned. "I guess I'm coming in."

"That's probably best."

Max greeted Jack with an outstretched hand and a wide smile. "Hey, man. We were just talking about you."

"I heard," Jack said. "Your father seems to know all about me."

"You were the topic of much conversation between the airport and here," Luna said, getting to her feet. "I'm Luna. It's so nice to meet you." She gave Jack an appraising look. "So … nice."

Jack felt like a piece of meat on a grill. "I … um … thanks."

"Stop trying to make him feel uncomfortable," Ivy said, slipping around Jack and moving back into the living room. "He's had a rough twenty-four hours. How is your Poison Ivy, by the way?"

"Is that what that is?" Max asked, leaning forward. "I was wondering. The guys down at the diner this afternoon said it looked like you had a hickey."

"I fell into some Poison Ivy yesterday," Jack said. "Ivy was nice enough to give me some lotion."

"Where is there Poison Ivy around here?" Max asked, making a face. "I don't want to risk running into it."

"It was out at her fairy ring."

Max straightened his shoulders and fixed Ivy with an incredulous look. "You took him to your fairy ring?"

"We took a walk," Ivy replied, irritated. She knew what he was insinuating, and she didn't like it. "We needed some air. He wanted to see the fairy ring. It's not like it's a big deal."

"If you say so," Max said.

Jack rubbed the back of his neck. "I really don't want to interrupt your reunion," he said. "I just have one quick thing to discuss with Ivy. If I can borrow her for a minute, I promise to give her right back."

"You can keep her if you want," Max suggested.

"I ... ."

"Ignore him," Ivy said. "He's purposely being a pain. What do you need?"

"Um ... are you sure you want me to tell you in front of your parents?"

"They're going to find out anyway," Ivy said. "They have ... ways ... of getting any information they want."

"Max?"

"Yup."

Jack snickered. "Well ... we identified the victim."

Ivy perked up. "You did? Who is she?"

Jack told Ivy about his afternoon, keeping the story as short as possible. When he got to the part about Chad, Ivy's pretty face twisted.

"Chad Hamilton? I haven't heard that name in years," Max said. "You really dodged a bullet with that one, pop tart."

"Stop calling me that," Ivy said before turning back to Jack. "Are you sure it's the same Chad Hamilton?"

"Brian seems to think so. I was hoping to get some insight from you before I drive up there tomorrow to talk to him."

Ivy rubbed her forehead, and Jack could practically see the conflict as it pressed down on her shoulders.

"You don't have to tell me anything if you don't want to," Jack said.

"It's not that," Ivy said. "I just ... I think I should go up there with you."

Jack was surprised. "You want to go up there with me? Why?"

"I don't know," Ivy admitted. "It's just a feeling. Do you have a problem if I go with you?"

"No," Jack said. "I ... I'm sure that will be fine. What about the nursery, though?"

"I guess I can shut it down for part of the day," Ivy said.

"I'll take care of it," Michael said. "Don't worry about it."

"I thought you were off until Monday?"

"I changed my mind," Michael said. "This sounds important. I think you should go up there. I'm kind of curious how Chad is doing these days."

"He was always such a nice boy before … well … before his troubles," Luna said. "I always hoped he would turn things around."

"It sounds like he's turning things around in a weird way," Max said. "He sounds … creepy."

"He does," Michael said. "That's why I'm glad Ivy won't be alone. She'll have Jack here with her."

"I guess that's right," Jack said, forcing a tight smile on his face. "So … we're going together?"

"Pick me up here tomorrow morning," Ivy said. "I'll fill you in on Chad during the drive."

"Okay," Jack said. "Can you be ready by seven?"

"Yes."

Jack moved toward the door. "I'll see you tomorrow morning."

"Oh, wait, what's your rush?" Luna asked. "You should stay for dinner."

"I'm not hungry," Jack said hurriedly. "I … this is your family time."

Luna ignored him. "What kind of dressing do you like on your salad?"

Jack sighed, looking to Ivy for help. "There's no way out of this, is there?"

"Just tell her what kind of dressing you like. She'll make things really uncomfortable if you try to fight her."

"Is it possible for things to be more uncomfortable?"

"You have no idea," Ivy said.

"So, Jack, tell me about your family," Luna said, smiling.

"You're not married, are you?" Michael asked.

Jack sighed and pinched the bridge of his nose. "I would love some ranch dressing."

Sixteen

"Your parents seem nice."

Jack picked Ivy up promptly at seven the next morning. Five minutes later he was struggling for a conversational topic that wouldn't leave them both feeling uncomfortable. It wasn't going well.

"They're good people," Ivy said. "They just don't respect other people's boundaries."

"They're nice," Jack said. "You're lucky to have them."

"I know," Ivy said. "They're just ... work."

"The best things in life often are."

"I guess."

They lapsed into silence for a few moments before Jack broke it. "Tell me about Chad Hamilton."

"He was a ... good guy," Ivy said. "I had trouble finding anyone who wanted to date me in high school, so when he started sniffing around, I was naturally suspicious. He turned out to be one of the good ones, though. At least at the start."

"Wait ... why did you have trouble finding dates in high school?"

"Look at me."

Jack was having trouble looking anywhere else. "You're very … attractive," he said. "Were you a late bloomer or something?"

Ivy shrugged, her cheeks coloring under Jack's compliment. "Not really. I mean … I don't think I looked particularly awful. I wasn't any great beauty, but I was … passable."

"Passable?"

"I don't know what you want me to say," Ivy said. "I was a normal-looking teenage girl. It is what it is."

"I don't believe you," Jack said. "There's nothing about you that's normal, including your looks. That's neither here nor there, though. Why didn't you date?"

"People thought I was weird," Ivy said. "Don't get me wrong, they still think I'm weird, but when you're weird in high school it turns people off. Chad was one of the few guys who bothered to look past the weird and try to get to know me."

"Why do you think that is?"

"I don't know," Ivy said. "That's a good question, though. I've never really thought about it. He was friends with Max … kind of … but I knew him more through school. One day it was just like he was always there. He was always asking about my day and trying to hold my hand and … well … finally, I gave in and agreed to go out with him."

"How long did you date?"

"We were together through half of our junior year and all of our senior year."

"So you were there when he tore his ACL?"

Ivy nodded. "Before he hurt himself, I used to think he was bigger than life," she said. "After, though, that's when I realized it was all an act. It was a good one, too. He had me snowed. Still, I convinced myself he was just going through a rough time and he would snap out of it.

"By the time spring rolled around and his baseball career was over, though, I knew he would never be the same boy he once was," she continued.

"When did you finally break up with him?"

"When I caught him sharing a tent with Maisie on the end-of-summer camping trip. Apparently it was cold and they had to huddle together in the same sleeping bag for warmth. Oh … and they were naked."

Jack frowned. "He cheated on you?"

"I think he did it more than once," Ivy said. "It doesn't matter. I *felt* like he was cheating on me before I actually caught him in the act. I was trying to find a nice way to break up with him, but I ended up with a messy one that was carried out in front of everybody."

"I'm sorry," Jack said.

Ivy shifted her gaze to him. "Why? You didn't do it."

"I know. It's still … that had to be rough."

"I was a teenager. Everything that happens when you're a teenager feels bigger than it usually is. I got over it."

Jack wasn't so sure. He had a feeling Chad's betrayal was one of the reasons Ivy was so standoffish. "I'm still sorry. If it's any consolation, I can't see how anyone would be stupid enough to cheat on you. That had to be one of the dumbest moves this guy ever made."

This time Jack didn't miss the blush rising up Ivy's cheeks. He knew flirting with her was a bad idea. He just couldn't seem to stop himself.

"DO ME A FAVOR AND STICK CLOSE TO ME," JACK SAID, surveying the expansive compound as he opened the passenger-side door of his truck. Without thinking what he was doing, he grabbed Ivy's hand as he helped her out – and the second their skin touched an electric current passed between them.

Ivy jerked her hand back, signifying Jack wasn't the only one who felt the jolt. "Chad wouldn't hurt me."

"You haven't seen him in years," Jack said, pressing his fingertips together absentmindedly. "You don't know what kind of man he is today."

"Are you going to be bossy?" Ivy asked, raising an eyebrow in challenge.

"Are you?" Jack shot back.

Ivy blew out a frustrated sigh. "I promise to stay close to you, master."

"You're cute," Jack said. "That 'master' crack only turns me on, though."

Ivy made a face. "Do you think that's funny?"

"I think your reaction is funny," Jack said, cracking a smile as his face softened. "Please, stay close to me. It will make me feel better."

"Fine," Ivy said. "I'm only agreeing because I still feel bad about the Poison Ivy, though."

"You should feel worse about saddling me with that dinner last night," Jack muttered.

"I heard that."

"You were meant to." Jack narrowed his eyes as he studied the compound. There were three rectangular buildings on the east side. They resembled barracks more than anything else. There were four large tents on the north side, and the fields to the west were tilled and ready for planting. There were a lot more than twenty people milling about, though. "How many people do you think are here?"

"It looks like more than fifty to me," Ivy said. "I ... this is creepy, right? Why are they all wearing robes?"

"I'm glad you think so, too," Jack said. "I don't want anyone accusing me of being judgmental."

"There are a lot more women here than men," Ivy said. "That has to be on purpose."

"It looks like all women out there working in the field," Jack said, pointing. "I have a feeling I'm going to stand out a lot more than you for once."

"Honey, you stand out wherever you go," Ivy said.

"Right back at you," Jack said. "I don't suppose you see your ex, do you?"

"Please don't call him that," Ivy said. "This place makes my skin crawl, and thinking he could have asked me to join him out here is totally freaking me out."

"I've got your back ... *honey*."

Ivy made a face. "Don't take it personally. I call everyone that."

"I've got it ... honey."

"You're unbelievable."

Jack grinned. He liked agitating her. When her feathers got ruffled she was even more beautiful, if that was possible. He opened his mouth to see how far he could push her, but the comment died on his lips when a young man stepped onto the path in front of them.

He looked timid and unsure at first, the blue robe setting off his angular features. After a few seconds of staring, though, he squared his shoulders and focused on the guests. "Can I help you?"

Ivy pasted a bright smile on her face. "Hi. My name is Ivy Morgan. We're looking for Chad Hamilton. Do you think you could point us in the right direction?"

Jack was impressed with her fortitude.

"Why do you want Chad?"

"We went to high school together," Ivy said, winking at the man and causing him to blush. "We're old friends. I heard he was up here and I just wanted to … visit."

The man narrowed his eyes. He looked suspicious, but Ivy was too pretty to deny. "Okay," he said finally. "You wait here, though. Interlopers are not allowed to wander around without an escort."

"Thank you … what is your name?"

"Heath."

"Thank you, Heath," Ivy said, practically purring. "We'll wait right here."

"Right there," Heath said, pointing for emphasis. "This is a sacred place. We won't risk you tainting it."

"I've got it," Ivy said, keeping her smile in place.

Heath left them with one more glance over his shoulder and then disappeared in the direction of the tents.

"It's a good thing I brought you," Jack said. "I don't think I would've gotten anywhere without your smile to entice him, honey."

Ivy tried to keep her face somber … but failed. For some reason, when he called her 'honey' – even though it was meant as a joke – her heart fluttered. "You think you're pretty charming, don't you?"

"Oh, honey, don't let my charm get you down," Jack teased.

Ivy rolled her eyes and turned back to the compound. "It seriously looks like the women outnumber the men by at least … what … four to one, doesn't it?"

"It does," Jack agreed. "Besides Heath … who wants to get in your pants, honey … I've only seen a few men. They're all young, too. I'm wondering if they're grandfathered in because they're the sons of some of these women."

"Do you really think Chad fancies himself a modern-day polygamist?"

"Brian floated that theory," Jack said. "I thought he was grasping at straws until I saw this place."

"And now?"

"Now I'm not so sure he wasn't right," Jack said. "I … wait …your love muffin is coming back and he's not alone."

"Why are you calling him that?" Ivy asked.

"Because the only reason he agreed to help us is because you're hot," Jack said. "I know my limitations, honey. I'm not ashamed to admit you're the one who charmed Heath."

"I didn't charm him. I smiled at him."

"I think you underestimate the power of your smile," Jack said.

Ivy's cheeks were burning again. Was he purposely trying to push her to the point where she was ready to rip his clothes off? "I … ."

"You're cute when you're flustered, honey."

"Stop saying that," Ivy hissed.

"Whatever you say … *honey*," Jack said, straightening his shoulders as Heath led a man in their direction. The long walk gave Jack a chance to study the robed man as he descended on them. His blond hair was long, flowing past his shoulders, and it was wavy in spots. He had an impressive beard, and as he closed the distance the smile he was boasting was a friendly one. There was still something behind his eyes that Jack didn't like. He just couldn't put a name to it. "Did he look like that when you were dating him?"

"He was a little less … mountain man."

"Brian said he thought he was trying to emulate Jesus Christ."

"Oh … wow … there it is," Ivy said. "That makes what he's got going on up here all the more creepy. It's as if he's trying to … pervert … a wonderful man's appearance."

"I think pervert is the right word," Jack said. "Make the introductions and then let me ask the questions."

"Yes, sir."

"I liked it better when you called me 'honey.'"

"IVY MORGAN. GIRL, YOU ARE A SIGHT FOR SORE EYES."

Chad greeted his former girlfriend with a friendly hug – one that seemed to trap her against his chest even as she struggled to step away. Jack didn't like it.

"It's good to see you, Chad," Ivy said. "It's been a long time."

"It has," Chad said. He still wasn't moving his hands from Ivy's arms, so Jack stepped in and grabbed her elbow, pulling her to him and away from the compound guru. Chad finally turned his attention to Jack. "And who are you?"

"I'm Jack Harker. I'm a police detective with the Shadow Lake Police Department."

"You're a long way out of your jurisdiction, detective."

"There are no boundaries on murder," Jack shot back. He had no idea why he was so irritated with Chad, but his proprietary attitude with Ivy probably had something to do with it.

"Oh, who has been murdered?"

"Mona Wheeler."

Chad didn't flinch. "Am I supposed to know who that is?"

"From what her parents say, she was a part of your little … group."

"I see," Chad said, rubbing his chin thoughtfully. "The name doesn't sound familiar. I'm sorry."

"You're denying knowing her?" Jack pressed.

"I'm afraid I am," Chad said. "I don't recognize that name."

He was lying. Jack was sure of it. "Can I question some of your other … followers? Is that what you call them, by the way?"

"We don't put labels on things here," Chad said. "It's not in our nature."

"Is that a yes or a no?"

"That's a no," Chad said. "We are a free community, and people are free to come and go as they please. If this … Mona … was here, she might have come and gone without me even realizing it."

"I'm not sure how that equates to you not allowing me to question your … friends," Jack said.

"We don't recognize the rules of your world," Chad said. "The problems of your society are not the problems of our society."

He sounded like a fortune cookie, which was enough to set Jack's teeth on edge.

"Come on, Chad," Ivy said, stepping in smoothly. "A young woman died. We have reason to believe she spent time up here. We're just trying to find out how she ended up in Shadow Lake."

"Ivy, it's only because of my great fondness for you that I haven't had you forcibly removed yet," Chad said. "If you wish to visit our society by yourself one day, I would be more than willing to give you a tour. If memory serves, you're open to alternative lifestyles."

Ivy licked her lips, unsure how to proceed. "But … ."

"Your friend and his … attitude … are not welcome, though," Chad said. "In fact, I'm going to have to ask you to leave right now. You're upsetting our balance."

Jack was about to upset something else when Ivy stilled him with a hand on his forearm. "We're going," she said.

Jack shot her an incredulous look. "We are?"

"Yes, honey, we are," Ivy replied, her eyes sending him a forceful message. "You don't have a warrant, and we really don't want to infringe on their religious rights. That would be a big no-no, wouldn't it?"

Jack growled. "I … ."

"We're going, Chad," Ivy said. "It was good to see you."

"It was good to see you, too," Chad said. "I forgot how beautiful in mind and body you were. My invitation stands, by the way. I'd love to spend some time with you when you *unshackle* yourself from this one."

"I'll consider it," Ivy said, tugging on Jack's arm. "We should really be going."

"Unshackle yourself, Ivy," Chad called to their retreating backs. "Open your mind. You won't regret it."

"I'm going to make him regret something," Jack grumbled.

Seventeen

"**W**hat are you doing?" Jack hissed, reaching for Ivy's ankle and trying to pull her back as she crawled up the hill.

"I want to see what they're doing," Ivy said. "Come on. You can't tell me you're not dying to watch them when they think no one is looking."

"Ivy ... ."

"Jack ... ."

Jack rolled his eyes. "This is technically illegal," he said. "We're breaking the law. They're freaks, but even freaks have a right to privacy."

Ivy sighed and rolled to her side, keeping her body pressed low as she regarded Jack. "I'm going to let you in a little secret," she said. "I've broken a law or two in my time."

"I never would have guessed," Jack deadpanned.

"I'm going to let you in on another little secret," Ivy said. "You have, too."

"I'm a police officer," Jack reminded her. "I don't break the law."

"Ever?"

"Ever."

"You're lying," Ivy said. "If you want to pretend you're some virtuous stick in the mud, though, go ahead."

"Following the rules does not make me a stick in the mud."

"You were going to hit Chad when you thought he hugged me too long."

"How can you possibly know that?"

"I read your mind," Ivy said, turning back to her crawling. "I am a witch, after all."

Jack was pretty sure she was messing with him, but part of him was torn. She had a way of knowing exactly what he was thinking – and it drove him crazy. It also intrigued him. "Fine," he said. "If we get caught, though, I'm blaming you."

"I grew up with Max," Ivy said, unruffled. "I'm used to that."

Jack grinned. "I'll just bet you two were hell on legs as kids."

"If you believe our parents, then yes. From their standpoint, we were awful."

"What about from your standpoint?"

"Honey, I'm an angel."

"Honey, something tells me you were a devil in angel's clothing," Jack said, crawling up next to her and angling his body so the low branches of a nearby tree hid him. "What do you see?"

"It looks like they're planting something in the field," Ivy said, pointing. "It seems a little early to me. I would wait two weeks to make sure it's not going to frost again."

"Brian seemed to think they were planting more than vegetables up here."

"If they are, they're not doing it in that field," Ivy said. "Chad isn't an idiot. He knows not to plant pot out in the open."

"Chad seemed like an idiot to me," Jack countered.

"You talked to him for five minutes."

"Any guy who would cheat on you is an idiot … honey."

Ivy rolled her eyes. "You should probably stop flirting with me if you don't want our impulses to get away from us again."

Jack stilled. He had been flirting with her. He just didn't expect her to call him on it. "I … do you want to talk about that?"

"Not really," Ivy said. "I prefer living in denial."

"Why?"

"The same reason you do," Ivy said. "I'm not looking for anything. I know you're not looking for anything. I think we're better off not looking for anything together. This constant flirting is going to get out of control if you're not careful."

"Meaning?"

"If you call me 'honey' one more time I'm going to rip your shirt off right here." They were bold words, but Ivy couldn't bring herself to meet Jack's serious gaze and back them up with a pointed glare. She didn't have the courage. She was afraid she would have to follow through on the threat if she lost herself in the molten chocolate depths of eyes.

"Noted," Jack said. "For the record, though, if I was looking for something ... I wouldn't look past you."

"Thank you."

"You're welcome." Jack waited. "Aren't you going to return the compliment?"

"Not right now, honey," Ivy said, her tone teasing. "Look over there. What do you think that is?"

Jack reluctantly tore his gaze from Ivy and focused on the back of the building she was gesturing toward. "They look like barracks," he said. "I think they sleep in there."

"Those are big buildings to sleep in. There has to be something else in there."

"I'm guessing Chad takes one of the buildings all to himself," Jack said. "He doesn't seem like a guy who likes to bunk down with others – unless he's going to have sex with them."

"And you're basing that on the conversation I just witnessed?"

"He wanted to initiate you into his harem," Jack said, his face serious. "If I hadn't been here ... I'm not sure what would've happened. I think he would've put the full-court press on you, though."

Ivy waited.

"That's a basketball metaphor."

"I know what a full-court press is," Ivy snapped.

"Oh, right, Max," Jack said. "I'm guessing he played a lot of sports in high school."

"I played basketball, too."

Jack was surprised. "On a team?"

"No. I didn't play well with others. I did play on the court at the high school with Max, though. I'm really quite good."

"You're *quite* good?"

"I'm amazing."

The double meaning of her words wasn't lost on Jack. The harder he fought her pull, the more he started to realize it might be a losing battle. He was almost ready to admit he wanted to lose. Almost. "We'll have to play one day," he said. "I'd like to see these mad basketball skills you're boasting about."

"Oh, we're going to play," Ivy said. "And when I win, you're going to owe me something big."

"Like?"

"Oh, I'm not going to tell you," Ivy said.

"Why? Are you afraid I'll lose on purpose?"

"What?" Ivy's cheeks colored when she realized what he was insinuating. "No more flirting."

"Then you need to follow your own rules," Jack said. "You were the one who flirted first this time."

"I was not flirting."

"Then what were you talking about?"

"I was going to make you weed my flower garden," Ivy sniffed.

Jack grinned. That was a lie. He didn't need to be a witch to know that. "I see. Well … I will happily weed your garden when you beat me at basketball."

"Good," Ivy said. "I hate weeding. I love planting, but weeding is a pain."

"What are you going to do for me when I win?"

"I guess I'm going to weed your garden," Ivy said.

"I don't have a garden," Jack said. "I might want something more … proactive … from you."

"See, that's flirting," Ivy said.

"I was talking about cleaning my house."

Ivy groaned. "You were not."

"How do you know?"

"Because I can read your mind."

"Is that a witch thing?" Jack asked.

"That's a woman thing."

The duo was so caught up in their verbal foreplay they didn't notice the robed figure detaching from the trees to their left. Heath was almost upon them before Jack's spatial impulses kicked in and he rolled over to put himself between Ivy and the interloper.

"What are you doing out here?" Heath asked accusingly. "This is private property."

"We were just … hunting for mushrooms," Ivy said, blinding Heath with a smile.

Heath furrowed his brow, although his face softened as he regarded Ivy. "Mushrooms?"

"It's morel season," Ivy said. "Jack here is a city boy. He's never been morel hunting."

"What makes you think there are morels here?"

"I've been hunting for morels since I was a kid," Ivy replied, refusing to back down. "I know where to look." Her eyes lit on familiar sight and she reached over and plucked the mushroom so she could hold it up for Heath's inspection. "See."

"But … why are you guys on the ground?"

"Well … ." Ivy racked her brain. "Jack was trying to get fresh. I was just explaining to him that I'm not interested. He's not taking it well. He fell to the ground, and I was trying to make him feel better so he wouldn't keep crying."

Jack scowled. "Really?"

"It's okay," Ivy said, patting his arm. She internally cringed when she felt the now familiar spark that always accompanied their shared touch. "You're not the first man to lose his mind over me."

"Obviously," Jack replied dryly. "I just met another one."

Now it was Ivy's turn to scowl. "Don't go there."

"I'm not the one who started it, *honey.*"

"It sounds like he has a crush on you," Heath said. "You should probably stop leading him on. It will just make things harder on him if you lead him on."

"You're right," Ivy said. "I often forget the power I have to make men fall in love with me."

Jack rolled over to his back and pushed himself into a sitting position. "You do have a certain … power."

"She's pretty," Heath said.

"She is pretty," Jack agreed. "She's also a rampant pain in the … ."

"You need to get out of here," Heath said, glancing over his shoulder. "If you're going to look for mushrooms, you should do it farther down the road. Chad won't like knowing you guys were up here."

"Then you probably shouldn't tell him," Jack said.

"I … ." Heath looked conflicted.

"Don't worry about it," Ivy said, drawing Heath's attention back to her. "We're going to go down the road. I need to find enough mushrooms to make my famous Alfredo. We won't keep looking here. I promise."

"I … you need to go," Heath repeated.

"We're going," Jack said, climbing to his feet. "Trust me. I've had just about all of this place as I can take."

Ivy shot one more reassuring smile in Heath's direction and then followed Jack down the hill. When it was just the two of them, Ivy directed the conversation to the pink elephant in the field.

"Chad has roving patrols checking to make sure no one is watching them."

"I figured that out, too," Jack said. "That definitely means he's up to something."

"What if one of those buildings isn't for sleeping," Ivy suggested.

"You think that's where he's growing pot?"

"It would make sense. He doesn't want anyone spying on him, and there are rumors of some nice bud being available for purchase out here. Of course, the field could be hidden in the woods and he could just be using the buildings to dry it."

Jack arched an eyebrow. "How do you know that?"

"I'm a naturalist witch," Ivy said. "People always assume I'm looking for herbal relief. You would be stunned at the drug offers I've gotten."

"I never thought of that," Jack said, rubbing the back of his neck.

"We still don't have enough for a search warrant. All we know right now is that Chad is creepy ... and we're fairly certain he's up to something. We have no idea what. Growing pot is one thing. I don't like it, but it doesn't tick me off like murder does."

"I still think he knew Mona," Ivy said. "It's been a long time, but I can tell when he's lying."

"Well, let's go back to Shadow Lake," Jack said. "I want to tell Brian what we've uncovered – even though it isn't much – and then I need to get some dinner."

"Speaking of dinner, we need to go and search those woods over there before we leave," Ivy said, pointing toward the opposite side of the road from where Jack was parked.

"Why? Do you think Chad is hiding something there?"

"I need morels," Ivy said, holding up the mushroom for emphasis. "I really do make a fantastic Alfredo pasta."

"Those things look ... gross."

"If you keep saying that I'm not going to give you any pasta."

"Maybe I don't want your pasta."

"Oh, you want my ... *pasta*," Ivy said, her eyes sparkling. "You don't want to want it, but you want it."

"I don't like mushrooms," Jack said, refusing to engage in the flirting. "I'm not big on pasta either."

"You're hunting for mushrooms, and that's the end of it," Ivy said, charging the rest of the way down the hill.

"You really are bossy," Jack called to her back.

She ignored him. It was just as well. If they threw any more veiled sexual comments at one another in the guise of food he was going to be the one ripping his own shirt off before reaching for hers.

This was getting out of control – and fast.

Eighteen

"How was your date yesterday?" Michael asked, watching Ivy as she settled on the ground and went to work on a hydrangea.

"It wasn't a date."

"I think it was."

"You need to stop listening to the crap Max is feeding you and realize that I'm not the dating sort," Ivy said. "I just … don't want to deal with it."

"I know you've had some bad luck in that department," Michael said. "Not all men are strong enough to handle a woman like you. That doesn't mean there aren't any out there. Look at your mother. She's not normal, and I've still managed to love her with my whole heart. You could find that."

"I'm not having this discussion."

"I like Jack," Michael said. "He seems like a standup guy."

"He's dealing with stuff of his own," Ivy said. "He's not looking for a relationship either."

"Maybe that means you two are perfect for each other."

"Or maybe it means we could do some real damage to each other,"

Ivy countered. "Dad, I love you. I know you just want me to be happy. I am happy, though. I don't need a man to complete me."

"I didn't say you did," Michael said. "I just ... you're looking for something, Ivy. You might not want to admit it. I see it, though. No, don't argue. I'm your father. I know you.

"Jack might not be what you're looking for," he continued. "I might be way off base. If I am, I'm sorry."

"Apology accepted."

Michael frowned. "I'm not way off base. You like him. The sooner you admit it the easier things will be on you."

"Stop it!" Ivy slammed her hands down on the ground, irritated. "Even if I wanted to pursue something with Jack, it's not an option. He has gone through something ... terrible. He's healing. He does not want a relationship. We're not right for each other."

Michael's face softened. "What do you mean he's gone through something terrible?"

"Something bad happened to him," Ivy said, her mind drifting to the scars on his chest. "I don't know what it is, but I do know it was truly awful."

"Maybe you can help him," Michael suggested.

"You can't help someone who doesn't want help," Ivy said, climbing to her feet and dusting off the back of her skirt. "Jack knows what kind of life he wants, and I'm not a part of it."

Ivy squared her shoulders and pasted a bright smile on her face for her father's benefit. "Now, I'm going to go over to the tree lot and see if anyone needs help. Are you good here?"

"I'm good," Michael said. He watched his daughter walk away from him, her head hung low. She'd always been good at lying to herself, but he could see she was starting to question those lies. He had no doubt Jack Harker was the reason why. Now he just had to figure out if Jack was really worthy of Ivy's heart because there was no way she could tolerate it being broken again.

He had an idea.

"THESE ARE BEAUTIFUL."

Ivy lifted her head from the small sapling she was pruning and almost fell over when her gaze landed on Chad and Heath. If she hadn't seen the two of them the day before she wouldn't have recognized them. Instead of the attention-grabbing robes, the men were dressed down in simple jeans and T-shirts. The robes must be relegated to home use, Ivy mused.

"Hi, Chad. I ... what are you doing here?"

"Well, after seeing you yesterday, I remembered that you opened a nursery," he said. "We've been looking for some trees to plant on the south side of the property, and I figured you would have some great stock."

"Sure," Ivy said, keeping her face neutral. "I can even give you a deal ... since we're old friends."

"Hi, Ivy," Heath said shyly.

"Hello, Heath," Ivy said, leery. *Did he tell Chad we were spying yesterday? Was that why Chad was really here?* "How are you today?"

"Good," Heath said. "I'm really good."

"That's great." Ivy decided to feign innocence. If Chad had the guts to question her about the spying she would tackle it then. "Do you know what kind of trees you're looking for?"

"I'm open to suggestions."

"I ... okay. Well, for that property, I think something that flowers might be beautiful. Since you guys are growing your own food up there, cherry trees would be a nice fit. You could eat the fruit and enjoy the blooms."

"That sounds like a good idea," Chad said. "I never would've thought of something like that."

"Well ... I aim to please."

"You always have," Chad said. "I ... um ... ." He glanced at Heath. "Could you give me a few moments alone with Ivy? We need to catch up, and I'd prefer doing it in private."

Heath shifted, crestfallen. "But ... ."

"I'm sure Ivy will grace you with her presence when we're done."

"Sure," Heath said. "I'll just look around."

"You do that." Once Heath was out of earshot Chad turned back to Ivy. "I can't tell you how good it is to see you. You look ... amazing."

Without an audience, Ivy was having a hard time holding on to feigned pleasantries. "You look like a reject from a bad Broadway revival."

"That's not very nice."

"I call it like I see it."

"I see you're still mad about my ... indiscretion ... on the camping trip," Chad said. "I really am sorry for what I did. I was lost during that time of my life. That's not an excuse, but I am sorry."

"It's been almost ten years," Ivy replied, nonplussed. "I'm pretty sure I'm over it."

"You don't seem like you're over it. I understand if you're still hurt. First love runs deep."

He was awfully full of himself. "You weren't my first love, Chad," Ivy said. "You were my first infatuation. There's a difference. You might think you crushed me when you slept with Maisie, but I already knew you'd cheated on me with at least three other girls. It wasn't quite the heartbreak you think it was."

Chad balked. "I ... how did you know?"

"People couldn't wait to tell me," Ivy said. "I was the weird girl who snagged the high school athletic god. People didn't understand it, and they couldn't wait to topple it."

"That's terrible," Chad said. "I had no idea."

"It doesn't matter," Ivy said, waving off his faux sympathy. "I was looking for a reason to break up with you when I stumbled upon you and Maisie. It was actually a relief."

"W-w-what do you mean?"

"We both knew we weren't in it for forever," Ivy said. "I just didn't want to be the bad guy and break up with you when you were going through so much. It was a decade ago, Chad. I've let it go. Don't worry that you somehow crushed me."

Ivy knew what she was doing when she made the admission. She was curious how he would react. She wasn't going to be disappointed.

"You were going to break up with me? I don't understand. That's just ... I was a catch. I was the best you were ever going to get."

There he is. There's the personality Chad always struggled to hide. Even before his life fell apart, he was there. Ivy just hadn't realized it until she was in so deep she could barely crawl out.

"I guess that's how you want to see it," Ivy said. "That's not how I see it. Now, how many trees do you want?"

"You wait just a second … ."

"MR. MORGAN?"

Jack studied Ivy's father with somber eyes and trepidation. When the man called asking Jack to stop by the nursery when he had a chance, Jack didn't know what to think. He was still confused. Michael hadn't left him with much room to argue, though, so here he was.

Michael brightened when he saw Jack. "You didn't have to rush out here," he said. "I know you're busy."

"You made it sound like it was important."

"It is," Michael said. "It's not more important than a murder investigation, though."

"We're still in the middle of things," Jack said, confused. "I had a few minutes. Is something going on? Did something happen to Ivy?"

Michael pressed his lips together, fighting the urge to smile. "I don't know. Are you going to make something happen to Ivy?"

Now Jack was really confused. "I … what?"

"Listen, son, I don't know you well, so I'm reluctant to broach a sensitive subject like this with you," Michael said. "The problem is, my love for my daughter outweighs any conversational norms I might ordinarily cling to."

"I don't understand."

"My daughter is struggling with … something … where you're concerned," Michael said. "She won't admit it. She's lying to herself. There's something about you that vexes her."

"Vexes?"

"She likes you."

"Sir … ." Jack was becoming increasingly uncomfortable. "I don't think this is something we should be talking about."

Michael ignored him. "She's warm for your form, boy. I don't know how you did it, but you've turned the woman who doesn't want anyone into the woman that won't admit she wants you."

"Sir, you seem like a good man," Jack said, forcing himself to remain calm. "You seem like a great father. Ivy and Max are a testament to something, and I have a feeling it's their upbringing.

"That being said, your daughter and I are not romantically involved," he continued. "She's not interested in me. As ... delightful ... as I find her, I'm not interested either. I'm not looking for a relationship."

"She told me."

"She did?"

"She told me all of that," Michael said. "She told me she's not interested in you and that you're not interested in her."

"Why am I out here then?"

"You're both terrible liars," Michael said. "I see the way you look at her, and she's just a bundle of energy right now. That's because of you."

"I don't know what you want me to say," Jack said. "I'm not lying to you. I'm not involved with your daughter, and I have no intention of changing that. I don't want to be involved with anyone."

Michael chuckled, the sound low and throaty. "I see you're just as stubborn as my Ivy," he said. "I guess I'm just going to have to leave you two to muddle through this on your own."

"We're not going to muddle through anything."

"You're lying to yourself, son," Michael said. "I guess that's your prerogative. This isn't any of my business. I promise to stay out of it from here on out. I just want to make you aware of one thing."

Jack waited.

"If you break her heart, I'll break your neck."

Jack was surprised by the threat, especially since Michael delivered it with a wide smile. "I have no intention of getting anywhere near Ivy's heart."

"Good enough," Michael said, shrugging. "I'm sorry to have interrupted your day. I hope you solve your case soon."

Jack did, too. The faster he could distance himself from Ivy and her crazy family, the faster he could claim the life he really wanted.

• • •

"TAKE your hands off me," Ivy warned, glaring at Chad as he gripped her elbow with enough force to whiten his knuckles. "I will hurt you if you don't."

"I don't think I like your attitude," Chad said. "I'm the man here. You need to treat me with respect."

Ivy attempted to rip her elbow away from Chad, but that only resulted in him digging his fingers in deeper. "Ow!"

"Apologize."

"Bite me," Ivy shot back.

"Apologize."

"Let me go right now!"

Ivy took an involuntary step back when Chad's grip suddenly eased. Before she realized exactly what was going on, Jack was between them and he had a harsh grip around the front of Chad's shirt. "Don't ever touch her."

Chad jerked away, casting a dark look in Jack's direction. "You."

"Me," Jack agreed.

"Don't ever put your hands on me," Chad said. "You won't like what happens if you do."

"Then don't put your hands on her," Jack said. "What are you even doing here?"

"I was going to buy some cherry trees," Chad said. "I think that ship has sailed."

"Good," Jack said. "Follow your ship to the parking lot and get your ass out of here. I'm not joking."

"Is this your property?"

"No," Jack said.

"Is she your property?"

"No."

"Then mind your own business," Chad said.

"Listen, I don't know what you think you're doing, and I don't know what you hoped to accomplish by coming here, but if you don't leave right now I'll arrest you," Jack threatened.

"On what charges?"

"Disturbing the peace."

Chad looked like he was going to argue further, but instead

straightened his shoulders. "You two need to stay away from my property, too," he said. "If I catch you spying out there again, I'll have you arrested."

Well, that answered that question. "Don't come back here, Chad," Ivy said. "You're not welcome."

"Oh, Ivy, don't let regrets about the past cloud your future."

"Oh, Chad, fire that fortune cookie writer who scripts your little platitudes," Ivy shot back. "They don't work on me."

Chad cast one more derisive look at Jack and then disappeared behind a row of trees. Once he was gone, Jack turned to Ivy. "Are you okay? Did he hurt you?"

Ivy rubbed her elbow. "I'm fine."

"Are you sure?"

"What are you even doing here?"

"I … ." There was no way Jack could tell her the truth. "I came out to see if you've gotten anywhere on the symbols."

"Not yet."

"Um … ."

"You could have called to ask me that," Ivy pointed out.

"I was in the neighborhood."

They lapsed into uncomfortable silence, which Jack couldn't take.

"Okay, well, keep me posted," Jack said. "I need to get back to the station."

Jack gave her a wide berth as he circled behind her and headed for the parking lot. His fingers were itching to touch her – he couldn't explain it – but there was no way he could stay on this path.

If he wasn't careful, Ivy Morgan was going to be the one thing that could change his life – and that was the one thing he couldn't allow. He wasn't good enough for her, and he wouldn't make the mistake of convincing himself otherwise.

She deserved better.

Nineteen

Ivy was still lost in her head when she left the nursery and turned toward home four hours later. Her father tried to engage her in conversation a few times over the course of the afternoon, but Ivy's stilted and uninterested replies finally told him the one thing he needed to hear: She wanted to be left alone.

The walk between Morgan's nursery and Ivy's house wasn't a long one, but Ivy opted for a meandering path so she could think. Chad's visit was the stuff of nightmares, and if she wasn't convinced he was hiding something before, she certainly was now. The question was: Was he trying to hide the fact that he was a murderer or a random pot grower with impulse control issues?

Once Chad found out Jack and Ivy were spying, his first inclination was to confront her. Sure, he'd gone about it in a roundabout way, but he'd never had any intention of buying cherry trees. He was trying to feel Ivy out. He wanted to know if she was suspicious, which she was.

His unfettered reaction to her disrespect was a whole other issue, and it was one Ivy wasn't in the mood to dwell on. All she wanted now was to eat her leftover pasta and curl up with a good book. She needed to escape to a different world because she wasn't overly fond of the one she was living in now.

Ivy was halfway up the front steps to her cottage when she noticed something on the front mat. She approached slowly, her eyes adjusting to the dimming light. It took her a moment, but she recognized the gift for what it was: a bouquet of flowers.

For a brief moment, Ivy's heart soared. *Was this why Jack was here? Did he leave flowers?* Ivy instantly hated herself for her reaction. She did not want Jack Harker. She didn't. He was off limits to her head and heart. She couldn't fool herself into thinking otherwise.

Ivy's hand was almost around the bouquet when her gaze shifted to the attached card. There was no writing on the envelope, and instead of picking up the flowers Ivy snagged the card and opened it.

Her heart hammered the second the pagan symbols from Mona's body swam into view. She still didn't recognize them for what they were, but she knew they were a warning. Jack definitely hadn't left the flowers.

Ivy turned swiftly, scanning the darkening woods that surrounded her house. She'd always felt safe here. This was her home. She was untouchable here. She couldn't help but feel as if someone was watching her, though.

With shaking fingers, Ivy drew her cell phone out of her pocket and punched in the number to the police station. She needed help – and something told her she needed it now.

JACK WAS A BUNDLE OF NERVES AS HE PULLED INTO IVY's driveway. He could see her pacing in front of the bay window, and his heart lodged in his throat as her lithe frame moved to and fro. She was beautiful.

She was also in trouble, he reminded himself.

Jack pocketed his keys and jumped out of his truck, glancing up when he heard the front door open. He increased his pace so he could get to her quicker, and he couldn't hide his surprise when Ivy threw herself into his arms.

He fought the urge to hold her – for exactly one second – and then tightened his arms around her and pulled her as close as he could manage without climbing inside of her skin. "Are you okay?"

"I ... ."

Jack pulled away, moving his hands up to cup the back of her head and force her gaze to his. "What's wrong?"

Ivy pointed at the flowers, her finger shaking. "I found those on the porch when I came home tonight."

Jack waited, and when Ivy didn't give any further information he hunkered down so he could study the bouquet. "They're flowers."

"I know that," Ivy said. "I ... this was with them." She handed the card to Jack.

He studied it briefly, his heart clenching when he recognized the symbols. He still didn't know what they meant, but one thing was clear: They were a warning. Someone was sending a clear message to Ivy.

"Do you think Chad left these?"

Ivy shrugged. "Who else?"

"You didn't see him leave them, though, right?"

"No."

Jack sighed, running his hand through his hair as he studied her expressive face. "You haven't seen anyone hanging around here, have you?"

"No."

"Okay." Jack knelt down. "I'm going to take these and ... ."

Ivy's hand darted out, stilling Jack. "Don't touch those."

"Why?"

"It's Windflower. It's poisonous. It will give you a rash ... and maybe something worse if you're not careful."

"Are you sure?"

Ivy rolled her eyes. "This is what I do for a living."

"I haven't forgotten," Jack said, straightening and holding his hands up to placate her. "I won't touch them. Let's go inside. You look a little shaken."

"Someone was here, Jack. Someone came to my home."

An invisible hand snaked around Jack's heart and squeezed it. She looked rattled. No, she looked terrified. It was something he never wanted to see on her face. "Come on, honey. Let's go inside."

There was no teasing in his words tonight.

"I NEED TO DO SOMETHING," IVY SAID, WALKING BACK AND forth in front of the counters in her small kitchen. "I need to think about something else. Food. Do you want food? I want food."

Jack wasn't hungry, but he was willing to agree to anything that would stop Ivy's relentless pacing. "I could eat."

"I made pasta last night. There's plenty leftover for both of us. I'll heat it up."

"Okay."

After leaving the flowers on the porch and calling Brian, Jack took photos and then watched as the older police officer confiscated the unsafe blooms and tossed them in his truck so he could transport them back to town.

After a brief discussion, Brian left Ivy in Jack's capable hands – and now Jack had no idea what to do. Ivy was a nervous wreck, and he felt like he might jump out of his skin at any moment. Being around her was turning him into a wreck, too – it was just a wreck of a different sort.

Jack watched Ivy work for the next twenty minutes, keeping his mouth shut and his eyes open. She knew what she was doing around a stove. Her hands were deft, and when she pushed the plate in front of him Jack was surprised to hear his stomach rumble in approval at the scent.

Maybe he was hungrier than he thought. "This looks good."

"I like to cook," Ivy said, sliding into the open chair next to him. "I … I didn't even ask if you're okay with this. I don't have any meat, but I might have some canned soup or something in the pantry if you'd rather have that."

"Why wouldn't I want this?"

"You said the morels looked gross."

Jack pressed his lips together, searching for the right words to make her feel better. He had no idea what they were. "Honey, I was just messing with you," he said. "I happen to love morels."

Ivy watched as he dug into the dish, her eyes wide. The mushrooms weren't what he was expecting – they definitely didn't taste like the ones dumped on his pizza whenever he ordered it – but they weren't half bad. "Delicious."

"You've never eaten morels before, have you?"

Jack considered lying and then changed his mind. "No. They're good, though."

"Do you want me to make you something else?"

"No."

"I … you're only still sitting here because you don't want to leave me alone while I'm freaking out," Ivy said. "The least I can do is cook you something you like. The problem is, I have no idea what you like."

"I like pasta," Jack said. "I like mushrooms. I like this. Please stop … doing that. If you keep this up, I'm going to start freaking out, and nobody wants to see that."

Ivy finally smiled, the first real one he'd seen since she threw herself into his arms on the front porch. It warmed him from the tips of his toes to the top of his head. God, he really loved her face.

Jack shook his head, jolting himself out of his melancholy. "What are you going to do when we're done here?"

"What do you mean?"

"Are you going to Max's house? Is he coming here?"

Ivy balked. "No. I'm not calling Max. I'm perfectly fine on my own."

Jack's warm feelings started to shift. "You're not staying here alone."

"Yes, I am."

"You are not," Jack said. "Someone could be watching you. There are thousands of places for people to hide in these woods. You're isolated here. If you get in trouble, I might not be able to make it out here in time to save you."

"Save me? I don't need anyone to save me."

The way she'd raced to him earlier told him differently. He decided to change tactics. "Ivy, it's okay to be afraid," he said. "Someone is threatening you. You should be afraid."

"I'm not afraid."

"You are, honey," Jack said. "I don't blame you. I'm scared for you. You can't stay here alone."

"Well, I am."

Jack growled, the sound taking both of them by surprise. He was done trying to be reasonable. "Fine. If you're staying here, then I'm staying here with you."

"No way," Ivy said. "I ... no. That's just asking for trouble."

Jack couldn't argue with the sentiment, but there was no way he was leaving her to her own devices. "You're either calling Max and having him come here, calling Max and going to his house, or finding a blanket and a pillow so I can sleep on your couch. Those are your options."

"You're not the boss of me."

"Don't push me on this, Ivy."

"Don't tell me what to do."

They narrowed their eyes as they faced off, both of them refusing to back down. It was anyone's guess who was going to win.

"I HOPE YOU'RE HAPPY."

Ivy hurled a pillow and blanket at Jack as he moved the back cushions from the couch to the floor.

"I'm thrilled," Jack said, refusing to make eye contact. He was convinced if he looked into her murderous eyes he was either going to shake her or take her. One of those emotions was going to get him into trouble. He just couldn't figure out which one.

"I want you to know that I'm lodging a formal complaint with the police chief tomorrow," Ivy warned.

"I'll be excited to read the report."

"I ... I don't need to be babysat."

"Good, because that's not what I'm doing," Jack said. "Quite frankly, I think those mushrooms were funky. My stomach is upset, and I'm really thankful you offered me a spot on your couch instead of risking me driving home when I have food poisoning."

"Are you suggesting I poisoned you with my cooking?" Ivy asked, hands on hips. Those were fighting words.

"I'm suggesting that no force on Earth could move me from this couch tonight," Jack said, reaching for the back of his shirt and tugging it over his head. She'd already seen the scars. There was no sense in hiding them now.

The second Ivy saw his muscled chest she knew she was in trouble. She had to get out of this room. They were both emotionally charged. They were either going to smack each other around or roll on top of each other naked. She couldn't tolerate either prospect. "I … ."

Jack kept his gaze trained on the couch. "Go to sleep, Ivy."

"Fine," she said. "I'm still not happy."

"At last you're safe."

Was she? She wasn't so sure. Every moment she spent with Jack put her one step closer to losing her heart. Losing her life was less scary.

Twenty

After a fitful night of tossing and turning, Ivy climbed out of bed grumpy the next morning. Her long hair was standing out in odd places, and her shorts and tank top were wrinkled. She didn't bother to fix any of it because she thought the sight of her in the morning would be just the thing to kill any inappropriate sexual interest – at least on Jack's part.

Unfortunately, the sight of him shirtless as he slumbered on her couch, his face peaceful and ridiculously handsome as it pressed against her pillow, only served to ratchet up her libido.

"Darn it," she grumbled, moving past the couch and heading straight for the kitchen so she could make a pot of coffee.

"Did you say something?" Jack mumbled into the pillow.

"I can't believe you look like *that* after you've slept for eight hours," Ivy said, not bothering to lie. "It's just not fair."

Jack opened his eyes, taking a second to focus on her as she buzzed around the kitchen and then fought to swallow his sigh. Her tiny shorts hung low on her hips and high on her thighs, making his mind swirl with fantasies about what was under them. Her tank top was simple, but it showed off her toned arms and back, and her face was devoid of makeup – but still beautiful. He even liked how her hair stood on end in places it wasn't supposed to.

In the harsh light of day, demanding to sleep on her couch seemed like a stupid idea.

"What's not fair?" he asked, rolling to a sitting position on the couch and cracking his neck. He couldn't drag his eyes from her thighs.

"You look like a model in the morning," Ivy said, flipping the switch on the coffee pot. "It's just not fair."

Jack chuckled. "I guess I'm supposed to take that as a compliment, huh?"

"I'm still mad at you," Ivy said, pushing her lower lip out. "You can take it however you want to take it. It's not my concern."

She was too cute for words. Jack's mind went to a dark place. It was incredibly hot, she was running her fingers through his hair, and … . "Um … what were you saying?"

"What were you thinking?" Ivy asked, narrowing her eyes.

"I wasn't thinking anything," Jack said, standing up and stretching. When he finished, Ivy's eyes were keenly focused on him – or rather the spot right above his boxer shorts. "What are you thinking?"

Ivy tugged a frustrated hand through her hair. "You don't want to know what I was thinking."

"I do."

"No, you don't," Ivy said. "Trust me."

Sadly, Jack was dying to hear what she was thinking. He had a feeling it matched what he was thinking. He shook his head to dislodge the thought. *Don't go there!* "We need to have a talk, Ivy."

"I don't want to talk to you," Ivy said. "I'm mad at you."

Adorable. That was the only word Jack could think of to describe her right now. No, that wasn't true. He could think of a few others. Sexy. Beautiful. Breathtaking. He was seriously getting sappy. This had to stop. "What can I do to make you forgive me?"

Ivy scowled at him. "Tell me you were wrong and I'm perfectly capable of taking care of myself."

"You're extremely capable," Jack said, choosing his words carefully. "You're … strong. That doesn't mean I was wrong. If something were to happen to you when I knew I could protect you, I would never forgive myself."

"Maybe I don't need to be protected," Ivy said, refusing to give in. "Maybe I was the one protecting you."

Jack grinned, charming her despite her foul mood. "Fine. We were protecting each other."

"I'm going to take it, but only because I'm too tired to argue with you," Ivy said. She pointed toward the kitchen table. "Sit down and I'll make you some breakfast."

"You don't need to cook for me," Jack said, although he was already moving. "I did kind of force myself on you last night."

"Yes, but I'm still a good hostess," Ivy said. "I have manners."

"Since when?"

"Sit down."

Jack smirked as he sat, running his hand over his stubbled chin as he watched her pull eggs, tomatoes, cheese and onions out of the refrigerator. "So, you're a vegetarian but not a vegan?"

"What do you know about either?"

"My sister is a vegan," he replied, unruffled. "She won't eat any cheese or eggs. She won't even use milk to cook."

"That's a little more restrictive than I can take," Ivy said, cracking eggs into a large mixing bowl. "I don't eat meat, but I do eat dairy products. Are you okay with an omelet?"

"Sure," Jack said. "I'm easy."

"What do you eat at your sister's house?"

"Nothing. Everything there tastes like feet."

Ivy snorted as she chopped up the tomato. "Some of the substitute products do taste a little funky."

"They taste like feet. Admit it."

"I haven't done a lot of feet eating."

Jack watched her, mesmerized as she dumped the eggs into a skillet and then started folding vegetables and cheese in. For one lonely moment, he pictured them sitting here every morning, chatting over breakfast after spending the night together. It was a cozy feeling. "Why aren't you married?"

Ivy balked. "Excuse me? Is this your usual level of morning chatter?"

"I'm sorry," Jack said, shrugging. "I just … you would make some guy really happy."

"On the contrary, I make men miserable," Ivy said.

"I don't believe that for a second," Jack said. "You've got a certain *way* about you. Men find you charming. Don't deny it. Brian told me every man in this town has tried to date you. He says you're the one fighting it."

"Men find me charming for about a month," Ivy said. "All of my Bohemian delights take about that long to wear off. Men like the weird girl from afar. When they actually get a chance to spend time with her they often find that they'd rather have a normal girl than put up with all the stares and whispers."

"I think most of that is in your head," Jack said. "I haven't seen anyone pointing and staring."

"Ava?"

"Ava has issues of her own," Jack said. "She's a bitter woman. She feels she always has to be in competition. She always wants to win, even if she doesn't really want the prize. That's a commentary on her, not you. Ava is the type of woman who will go after anyone she deems competition. It's not about you being different. It's about men wanting you more than they want her."

Ivy's mouth dropped open.

"You're going to catch flies if you're not careful," Jack said.

Ivy turned back to the stove and pulled the skillet off, dividing the omelet in two and handing half of it to Jack before settling in the spot next to him at the table. Jack dug in with gusto while Ivy watched him eat. "Why aren't you married?"

Jack swallowed, meeting Ivy's probing gaze. "I'm not husband material."

Ivy didn't believe him. "Why?"

"I'm a cop," he replied. "I keep odd hours. I'm dedicated to my job. There's always a chance I won't come home at night."

"There's a chance we all won't come home at night," Ivy said. "And you're not in the city anymore. This is the first murder Shadow Lake has seen in – I can't remember the last one. You'll be able to keep more regular hours around here. What else do you have?"

Jack focused on his plate, worried that if he met Ivy's sea-blue eyes he would jump in and drown himself in their beautiful depths. "I don't have anything to give anyone else right now," he said. "I … am dealing with some other stuff, and a relationship takes give and take. I have nothing to give."

Ivy's heart rolled sympathetically. "Okay."

Jack arched an eyebrow. "Okay?"

"You're honest," Ivy said. "You know your own limitations. I admire that. I have the same limitations."

"I think you're limiting yourself," Jack countered. "You hide out here because you think people are looking at you a certain way. Trust me, Ivy. They're not looking at you with anything other than marvel and envy."

Ivy made a face. "Thank you for saying that," she said. "I don't believe it for a second."

"WAIT! Don't put your shirt on yet."

After showering and shaving with one of Ivy's disposable lady razors (something that should have embarrassed him – and yet didn't) Jack was readying himself to leave. Before that happened, though, he needed to have a serious discussion with Ivy – and he wasn't looking forward to it.

"Why can't I put my shirt on?" Jack asked dryly, arching an eyebrow. "Are you ready to give in to an impulse?" He had no idea why he said it. Part of him was hoping she would say yes, though.

Ivy rolled her eyes, her long hair damp from her own shower as she moved closer to Jack. "Sit down."

"Why?"

"Sit down, please."

"Why?"

"Sit down or I'm going to make you sit down," Ivy threatened, brandishing a tube of lotion as she regarded him with a serious expression.

"Fine," Jack said, slouching on the armchair. "What?"

"This is a special lotion," Ivy said, squirting a dollop onto her hand and then transferring it over to Jack's scars.

He squirmed at the contact, opening his mouth to protest, but Ivy cut him off.

"You'll always have the scars, but this will help them fade," she said. "Put it on in the morning after you shower and at night before you go to bed. In a month, they'll be a lot less obvious."

"Maybe I want them to be obvious." The feeling of Ivy's fingers on his chest was driving Jack to distraction.

"You're scarred in here," Ivy said, pressing her fingertips to the spot above his heart. "You don't want them to be obvious. That's why you didn't want to take your shirt off the other night. You're embarrassed, but I have no idea why."

"I'm not embarrassed."

"You are. It's okay. You still don't have to tell me."

"I ... I was shot." Jack swallowed hard.

"I know."

"Don't you want to know why?"

"No."

"Why not? Everyone wants to know why."

"You're not ready to tell me," Ivy said pragmatically. "When you're ready, you'll tell me. I won't have to ask."

"That's it? You're just going to let it go?"

"Yup," Ivy said, straightening as she handed him the bottle of lotion. "I made that myself. It's my last bottle. I'll make more. It will be ready when you need it."

"You make lotion?"

"I'm multitalented."

"I've noticed," Jack mumbled. "I ... we need to talk about the flowers." He was running as far away from this conversation as he could get.

"We both believe Chad left them," Ivy said. "What are you going to do about it?"

"I'm going to go in front of a judge and see if I can get a search warrant for Chad's compound," Jack said. "What I want to know is if you're going to be okay if I leave you here."

"I'm a big girl, Jack," Ivy said. "I can take care of myself."

"I didn't say you couldn't, honey," Jack said. "I just ... the world would be a worse place without you in it. Promise me you're going to be really careful."

"I promise."

"What are you going to do today?"

"I need to find what those symbols mean," Ivy said. "They haunted my dreams last night. I know I've seen them before."

Jack reached over and grabbed her hand, directing her attention to him. "Don't go out to Chad's compound. Don't wander around the woods alone. Drive over to the nursery. Lock yourself in this house before it gets dark. Keep your cell phone close to you in case someone tries to break in."

"I ... ."

"Promise me."

"I promise."

"Good," Jack said, squeezing her hand and then letting it go. "I still believe there's a weird happy ending out there for you. You need to live to see it, though."

He didn't add that he desperately wished he could be involved in that ending. It was a moot point. He didn't have anything to give her, and she deserved the moon, the stars, and everything in between.

Twenty-One

"This is pretty thin."

Judge Walter Cunningham looked over the documents spread out on his desk in front of him dubiously.

"I understand that, sir," Brian said, exhaling heavily. "It's what we have, though, and after last night I'm not sure I feel comfortable with him running around."

Cunningham rolled his eyes. "We went to school together, Brian. You don't have to call me 'sir.'"

"You're a judge."

"Your mother once made us take a bath together because we got filthy in a mud pit after a thunderstorm," Cunningham said.

"We were children."

"We were eight," Cunningham said. "I'm still scarred. Don't call me sir. It bugs me."

"Fine, Walt," Brian said. "We need to do something about Hamilton. You see that, right?"

"How sure are you that he's a murderer?"

"Very," Brian said.

Cunningham shifted his gaze to Jack. "How sure are you?"

Jack shrugged. "I'm pretty sure. He was clearly trying to hide something when we were up there, and for him to come down here and immediately go after Ivy Morgan ... well ... that has to mean something."

"No one saw him put the flowers on Ivy's porch, though," Cunningham pointed out. "We don't know that it was him."

"Who else?" Jack asked, agitated. "He went after Ivy at the nursery and the flowers were waiting for her when she got home. That can't be a coincidence."

"I agree," Cunningham said. "I just ... we still have no direct evidence that points to the victim spending time at Hamilton's compound."

"Her parents said she kept talking about him," Brian said.

"That's not proof," Cunningham said. "No one saw any contraband up there, right? No pot?"

Jack shook his head. "Ivy said that Chad was too smart to plant pot out in the open," he said. "She thought it might be in one of the buildings, but we obviously didn't get a chance to search it."

"And why did Ivy Morgan go to question Chad with you again?"

Jack blanched. "I ... ."

"I suggested that Ivy might have insight into Chad that we didn't have," Brian said. "She dated him for a year."

"And then she publicly dumped him when he tripped and fell into Maisie," Cunningham said. "Oh, don't look surprised, Detective Harker. I may be a judge, but I still keep up on the gossip in Shadow Lake. I happen to be good friends with Michael Morgan."

"He just got back into town the day before yesterday," Brian said. "We should call him to get our weekly poker game back going."

"We should," Cunningham agreed. "Have you seen him?"

"Not yet."

"I have," Jack said, immediately wishing he could pull the words back into his mouth.

"You've seen Michael?" Cunningham asked, arching an eyebrow. "How?"

"I ... um ... he was at Ivy's house the night I went to talk to her about Chad," Jack said, opting to leave out their interaction from the previous afternoon. "Her mother invited me to dinner ... although 'insisted' is probably the better term."

Cunningham smirked. "That sounds like Luna." He studied Jack with serious eyes. "Are you and Ivy ... ?"

"We've just had occasion to bump into each other a few times," Jack replied stiffly. "We're not involved."

Cunningham and Brian exchanged an amused look.

"We're not," Jack repeated.

"I believe you," Cunningham said, holding up his hand. "Okay, here's what I'm going to do: I'm going to give you a search warrant for items in the Mona Wheeler case. We're looking for her personal belongings. If you happen to stumble over some pot, that would be great. That would allow me to extend the warrant to everyone on the compound."

"What about the threat to Ivy?" Jack asked.

"We don't know Chad is responsible for that," Cunningham said. "For now, this is the best I can do."

"I guess we'll take it," Jack said. "I'll meet you out by the car, Brian."

Once he left the room Cunningham let loose with the laugh he was trying to swallow. "That boy is a goner."

"Ivy is just as bad," Brian said. "They're like bickering little high-schoolers. There are hormones flying in every direction."

"That's interesting," Cunningham said. "I've never understood why Ivy is single. Every man in this town who isn't already married has a crush on her."

"I wouldn't pick out wedding gifts just yet," Brian said. "These two are going to fight it for as long as they can. When they finally do give in, it's going to be like an explosion."

"That sounds fun," Cunningham said, signing the search warrant. "Keep me updated."

"I'll tell you what we find at the compound," Brian said.

"I wasn't talking about the compound," Cunningham said. "I'm dying to find out what happens between Detective Harker and Ivy. That whole thing has piqued my interest."

"You're like a little old woman," Brian said.

"I like gossip," Cunningham agreed. "Now, go and get our murderer. I would really like Ivy Morgan's dating status to be the biggest thing going on in town by the weekend, if at all possible."

"You and me both."

"PLEASE TELL ME YOU HAVE SOMETHING," IVY SAID, PUSHING her way into Felicity's store and plopping down on one of the stools with a dramatic sigh.

"Good morning to you, too, niece," Felicity said, barely raising her eyes. "Why are you so … fluttery … this morning?"

"I'm not fluttery."

"You are," Felicity said. "Your aura is darker than normal."

"Maybe I'm just in a bad mood. By the way, that aura thing is a cool gift to have. Telling people about it is annoying, though."

Felicity chuckled. "You really are in a bad mood. What's wrong? Are you and Jack still fighting?"

"Define fighting."

"Yelling and scratching at each other."

"I did some yelling last night."

Felicity waited.

"I forgave him this morning," Ivy said. "He can't help himself. He's just bossy by nature."

This time Felicity guffawed. "He spent the night?"

"On the couch," Ivy said. "I had kind of a situation last night." Ivy told her aunt about the previous few days, and when she was done, her aunt was all business.

"That is not good," Felicity said. "I always knew there was something wrong with that Hamilton boy. Didn't I tell you there was something wrong with him?"

"You're wise and beautiful," Ivy deadpanned.

"How did he look?"

"Like he was trying to pretend he was Jesus Christ," Ivy said. "He's got this long beard, and his hair is all … snarled and stuff. He also wears robes around. Although, when he came to the nursery yesterday, he was dressed in street clothes."

"Probably because he didn't want to stand out," Felicity said. "He knew robes would draw attention to him. Even though your cottage is set back from the road, someone might have noticed a freak in a robe wandering around."

"I never thought of that," Ivy said, rubbing the back of her neck. "I'm more concerned with the symbols on the flowers. Have you found anything?"

"As a matter of fact, I have," Felicity said.

"Why didn't you call?"

"Because I just found it this morning," Felicity said. "Take a chill pill."

"I hate that saying."

"I hate your attitude right now," Felicity said. "You're a bundle of nerves."

"That's because someone left a threatening note with poisonous flowers for me on my front porch last night."

"That's only part of it," Felicity said. "You're more upset because Jack slept at your house and you had dirty thoughts about him all night."

"That is not true!"

"I'm your aunt," Felicity said. "I know you. Don't bother lying to me."

"I don't know what it is with everyone in my life, but I don't have feelings for Jack Harker," Ivy said. "He's just a police detective I'm being forced to spend time with."

"Your nose is growing."

"I … shut up."

Felicity sighed and finally focused all of her attention on her niece. "It's okay to like him. He's an attractive man. He's also very pleasant and smart."

"He's not looking for a relationship. Neither am I."

"You don't have to be looking. One just might find you both."

"Whatever," Ivy said. "I'm not having this conversation again. What did you find on the symbols?"

"I'm going to let this go, but only for now," Felicity said. "A murder investigation is more important than your love life. Once it's solved, though, you and I are going to have a very long chat about your attitude."

"I can't wait."

"About the symbols, though, there's a reason we thought they looked familiar but we didn't recognize them," Felicity said. "I ran them through my computer program, and since I've scanned most of my text and reference books I expected to find a hit there. When I didn't, I got frustrated.

"Just like you, I knew darned well I'd seen those symbols before," she continued. "On a whim, I opened the search up to all the books I've scanned. That's when I got a hit."

"I'm waiting for the big reveal," Ivy said. "It's like I'm on a soap opera. The only thing we're missing is the dramatic music and people talking to themselves out in the open."

Felicity made a face. "Sleeping with Jack might do wonders for your attitude, missy."

"I'm sorry," Ivy said, holding up her hands in mock surrender. "I didn't sleep well last night. I'm tired and grumpy. That's not your fault."

"I still think you should sleep with Jack."

"Auntie ... ." Ivy was exasperated.

Felicity graced her with a soft smile. "The symbols are from *The Covenant*."

Ivy frowned, racking her brain. "I ... what is that?"

"It's that book you brought to me when you were in high school," Felicity said. "Don't you remember?"

"You're going to have to be more specific. I brought you hundreds of books."

"It was the one I was upset about," Felicity said.

Ivy furrowed her brow. "The one with all the sex?"

"I wasn't upset about that book."

"You confiscated it."

"That's because I wanted to read it," Felicity said. "I just didn't want you to think I was a pervert. You were at an impressionable age. This is the one that you thought was a real pagan text, but it turned out to be fiction."

"Oh," Ivy said, her expression thoughtful. "I forgot all about that book. I remember I was upset because I thought it was real. It had all those symbols in it, and it was talking about Wicca like it was a way to excuse doing evil things to one another. You were the one that pointed out it was just fiction masquerading as non-fiction."

"There were some dangerous ideas in that book," Felicity said. "That's why ... well ... I guess I shouldn't have been surprised that someone tried to take the ideas from that book and pervert them for their own means ... but this is something else."

"Did you find out what the symbols mean in the book?"

"Well, that's also interesting," Felicity said, moving behind her laptop and pressing a few buttons. "See here? From what I can tell these symbols are basically nonsense – other than the fact that all of them have to do with sex in the book. Do you remember what symbols you got on your card?"

"The same ones."

"That means someone is looking at you in a sexual manner."

"I ... are you sure?"

"I'm not sure," Felicity said. "I just know that a girl was found dead in your yard and she had these symbols carved into her body. Now you've gotten a card with the same symbols. Someone is clearly interested in you."

"Chad?"

"I have no idea," Felicity said. "You know very well I'm not clairvoyant. Your gifts are stronger in that arena, even though you refuse to use them. We still need to have a conversation about that, by the way. You need to be very careful until this is sorted out, though."

"Maybe I should ask Max to stay with me," Ivy mused, tension building in her shoulders.

"You could ask Jack."

"You're no longer my favorite aunt."

Felicity shrugged, unruffled. "Ask him. I think it might be fun. It will probably help with that grumpy thing you've got going on."

"And, on that note, I'm leaving."

"Take the book to Jack when you go," Felicity said. "It will give you an excuse to see him without looking desperate."

"I really hate you sometimes."

"I love you, too."

Twenty-Two

"Have a seat, Mr. Hamilton."

Chad's expression was murderous as he regarded Brian and Jack with utter hatred. After delivering the search warrant to the compound, the investigators searched the barracks. And while they didn't find a bounty of pot like they were hoping, they did find Mona Wheeler's wallet hidden under a pile of clothes. It wasn't much, but it was enough to get the extended search warrant and take Chad in for questioning.

Jack was taking it as a win. Now he just had to break Chad. He was up for the challenge.

"I don't recognize your authority," Chad said. "You have no power over me."

"Great," Jack said, nonplussed. "Take a seat. You're going to be here for a little while. You might want to get comfortable."

"I'm fine standing."

"Suit yourself," Jack said, flipping through his file. "Mr. Hamilton, can you explain why Mona Wheeler's wallet was found on your property?"

"I'm not answering your questions."

"That's your prerogative," Jack said. "Why don't we tell you what we suspect and go from there. How does that sound?"

"It sounds like you're trying to infringe on my religious rights."

"Let's start with the fact that Mona Wheeler's parents told us she was spouting some of your ... platitudes ... on visits home over the past few months. Can you explain that?"

"They're not platitudes," Chad snapped. "They're tenets of our faith."

"Can you explain this whole ... passengers ... thing to me?"

"Who told you about that?" Chad asked, his eyes narrowed.

"Mona told her parents."

"I ... that's why she was banned from our group," Chad said. "She didn't follow the rules. She was incapable of it."

If Jack didn't know better, he would think the compound guru was talking to himself. "When was Mona banned?"

Chad scowled. "A few weeks ago. She kept telling absolute strangers about our faith. It was like she was bragging. We don't brag at Covenant."

Jack frowned. "What is Covenant?"

"That's the name of our home," Chad said.

"Who named it that?"

"God."

Brian and Jack exchanged a look.

"I see," Jack said. "Does God talk to you?"

"God talks to all of us if we open our hearts," Chad said, sinking into a chair and embracing what could only be described as a masterful performance. "Have you considered opening yourself to God, Detective Harker?"

"Sure," Jack said, not missing a beat. "I would love to open myself to God. Do I have to be a passenger to do it?"

"You don't even understand what you're saying," Chad seethed. "Human beings cannot be passengers. Passengers come from another world. They were never born of this one."

"Well, that sounds fun," Jack said. "Are you a passenger?"

"I am the Promise."

"The promise of what?"

"The future."

"I don't know what that means," Jack said.

"That's because you're not enlightened," Chad said. "You're of this world. You cannot understand the fathomless energy of all the others."

"You just spout nonsense out of your rear end these days, don't you?" Brian interrupted the conversation. "I know your parents, Chad. You were born of this world, too."

"That's just the lie they told to cover up the miracle of my birth."

"You've flipped your lid," Brian said. "It's sad. I know what happened to you as a teenager threw you off course, but this is just … ."

"He doesn't believe it," Jack said.

"Of course I believe it," Chad snapped. "I am the Promise."

"You're running a scam," Jack countered. "You've managed to convince a whole bunch of people – most of them female, mind you – that you're something special. You've created a religion that allows you to live off the grid. That's how you like it.

"You have other people doing all the work," he continued. "They plant the fields. They irrigate them. They harvest them. Meanwhile, you sit around on your paper throne and pretend you have some insight into the grand scheme of things.

"You target women who you think are going to be easily manipulated," Jack said. "You convince them you have the answers about an afterlife, which is something they're desperate for. I'm guessing you use your power to get them into bed. Are you trying to father a bunch of kids? Or is the sex enough on its own?"

Chad slammed his hand down on the desk. "Don't you dare blaspheme my faith."

"Shut up," Jack snapped. "You're not fooling me. Personally, I don't care what you're doing up there as long as you're not doing it to kids and you're not ripping people off. It's not my problem.

"What I am interested in is Mona Wheeler," he continued. "Why did you kill her?"

"I didn't kill her," Chad said, his voice plaintive. "I would never do something like that."

"You banned her."

"Only because she kept telling people our secrets," Chad said.

"Honestly, I liked Mona. She had a lot of … energy."

"Meaning you had sex with her," Jack said. "Nice."

"No one is forced into anything," Chad said. "Everything is voluntary. We only give people who are interested in our faith, and who have passed the first five rungs of ascension, tours. I'm not stupid. Mona was well on her way … and then she fell off the wagon."

"What happened?"

"We found out she was down at the local high school trying to recruit people," Chad said. "That's not how we work."

"What did Mona do when you told her she was banned?"

"She pitched a fit," Chad said. "She said she was going to tell everyone that we were doing freaky sexual rites up at the compound."

"Were you?"

"Absolutely not," Chad said. "Given the rules of our faith, only the Promise is allowed to engage in sexual acts."

"That's why there are so few men up there," Brian said. "Men are less likely to forego sexual gratification than women."

"I gratify the women," Chad said. "Don't you doubt it."

He was boastful. He was used to women falling at his feet. It started when he was a teenager, Jack realized. Once he lost his athletic scholarship his popularity started to fade. This was the idea he'd come up with to put himself back on a pedestal. "Why did you go after Ivy? She's never going to be malleable enough to be a member of your harem."

"I didn't go after Ivy," Chad said. "I talked to her. There's a difference."

"You grabbed her and threatened her," Jack countered. "That's going after her."

"She said some nasty things to me that were completely untrue," Chad said. "I never threatened her."

"You seemed interested in giving her a tour of your compound."

"She's hot," Chad said, shrugging. "She's always been hot. She's also open to alternative ways of living, and she doesn't cast stones. I thought she might want to expand her horizons."

"You thought she might give the Promise another shot in the sack," Jack said. "At least be honest."

"Fine. She's hot. She's a complete and total bitch, though. She told me she was never in love with me. Can you believe that?"

"Quite easily," Jack said, causing Brian to snicker.

"She was in love with me," Chad said. "I crushed her when I broke up with her. She's still pining for me."

"She broke up with you," Brian said. "She caught you using your little … promise … with Maisie. Every teenager in town saw her dump you."

"Whatever," Chad said. "The gossip mill in this town is absolutely ridiculous."

"You're ridiculous," Jack said. "Why did you leave those flowers on Ivy's porch last night? Was it a threat? Were you planning on going back to her house after you scared her a little bit?"

"What flowers?"

"Don't do that," Jack said, extending his finger. "The symbols carved into Mona Wheeler's body were the exact same symbols on the card. We know it was you."

"You don't know what you're talking about," Chad said. "I would never go after anyone. I would never murder anyone."

"You still haven't told us what happened when you told Mona she was banned," Brian pointed out.

"She freaked out," Chad said. "She yelled at me and called me a fraud and then she said she was going to leave that night. That's the last time I saw her. I swear."

Jack didn't believe him. He was spinning an elaborate story – but it was still a story. There was very little truth to his words. "I … ."

The sound of someone knocking on the office door – Shadow Lake was too small for an interrogation room – caused Jack to shift his attention. Ivy was on the other side, and he could see her peering in through the small window. "What the … ?"

"I've got her," Brian said, getting to his feet.

"Are you going to let her come in here and be mean to me again?" Chad asked. "Is that why she's here?"

"Shut up," Jack said, rolling his eyes.

Brian let Ivy into the room. She was excited, and she was clutching a book close to her chest. "I know what the symbols are."

Jack lifted his eyebrows, surprised. "You figured it out?"

"Aunt Felicity did," Ivy conceded.

"Ivy, do you want to call your guard dog off?" Chad asked, fixing her with a look. "He's jealous of our relationship. That's why he brought me in."

"I told you to shut up," Jack said before turning back to Ivy. "What do the symbols mean?"

"May I?"

Jack took a step back and let her move over to the table. He kept an eye on Chad. The man would never get his hands on her if he lunged, Jack would make sure of that, but he still wasn't taking any chances.

"The symbols weren't from reference books," Ivy said. "They were from a fiction book called *The Covenant.*"

"Well, that's interesting," Jack said, shooting a look at Chad. "Your ex-boyfriend here just told us the name of his compound was Covenant."

"Don't call him that," Ivy said. "You know I don't like it."

"I'm sorry, honey."

"Stop that, too."

Jack rolled his eyes until they landed on Brian, who was smirking in his direction. Jack immediately stiffened his shoulders. "What about the symbols?"

"Well, as far as we can tell, they're mostly nonsense," Ivy said, opening the book to the page Felicity marked. "All the symbols carved into Mona's body – and the ones left at my house – are of a sexual nature."

"Go figure," Jack said. "Chad is the only one at the compound allowed to have sex."

"Is that why there are no other men?"

"Yup."

"You're a pig," Ivy said, glaring at Chad.

"You're just jealous that they get my attention and you don't," Chad said. "Admit it."

"Chad, you were bad in bed when we were teenagers," Ivy said. "Now that you think you're king of the hill, I'm betting you're worse.

Now … shut up and let the adults talk." She patted his head condescendingly, forcing Jack to snag her hand and move her away from Chad.

"Don't touch him," Jack scolded.

"Why? Do you think he'll hurt me?"

"It's just tacky."

Ivy smirked. "Has he admitted to killing Mona?"

"He says it wasn't him."

"What about leaving the flowers and note for me?"

Jack shook his head. "He says no."

"Do you believe him?"

"What do you think?"

"I think you should lock him up and throw away the key," Ivy said.

"Do you know what your problem is, Ivy?" Chad asked. "You're a bitter woman. Losing the great love of your life has closed you off to the possibilities of life. Do you have a close relationship with God?"

"If you don't stop doing that I'm going to thump you," Jack warned.

"And I'm going to turn around and pretend I don't hear," Brian said. "Just … shut up, Chad. You're not doing yourself any favors."

Chad crossed his arms over his chest. "Are we done here? I need to get back to the compound. I have a schedule to keep, and if I screw it up all of my women fight over me."

"There's not much to fight about," Ivy said, holding her index finger and thumb about an inch apart for emphasis.

"That's a lie," Chad hissed.

Jack shook his head to still Chad when he reached for his belt. It almost looked as if he was about to put on a show for Ivy's benefit. "Don't even think about it."

"I'm leaving," Chad said, getting to his feet.

"No, you're not," Brian said. "You're here for questioning, and we're not done asking questions yet."

"Fine," Chad said, wrinkling his nose. "Then I want a lawyer."

Jack and Brian glanced at each other, deflating. If Chad was going to lawyer up, this was going to be a much longer night than either one of them was initially anticipating.

Twenty-Three

"Why are we out here?"

Jack held the back of Ivy's neck so she didn't barrel back into the office and start railing Chad with questions again. "Because he requested a lawyer."

"So?"

"So he's got a right to representation," Jack said. "Stop squirming."

"Don't tell me what to do."

"If you don't stop squirming I'm going to tie you to a chair," Jack said.

"You're such a ... ."

"Great detective?"

"I was going to say bully," Ivy said, crossing her arms over her chest. "You're a big bully."

"You're too cute for words." Jack realized too late he'd said the words out loud. He cleared his throat, avoiding Ivy's probing gaze, and focused on the book in her hands. "Can I hold on to that?"

Ivy handed the book over to him wordlessly.

"Thank you for bringing this here. You helped us a great deal," Jack said. "You should probably go home now, though."

"But ... I want to watch you put the screws to Chad."

Jack smirked. "You watch too much television."

"I watch very little television. I watch *Game of Thrones*, *The Walking Dead* and *Hannibal*. That's it."

"That's some pretty eclectic taste there."

"I watch *Game of Thrones* because I like dragons. I watch *The Walking Dead* because I like Norman Reedus. He's beyond hot."

Jack internally scowled. He had no idea who that was, but he already didn't like him. "Why do you watch *Hannibal*?"

"I like to cook."

Jack made a face. "Nice. I'm never eating anything at your house again."

"Like I would invite you," Ivy muttered.

"We'll talk about that later," Jack said. "You should really go home now, though. This could go on for a long time."

"But … I want to know why he did it."

"I'm not sure he's ever going to come through with the answers you're looking for," Jack said. "He said that Mona was banned from the group because she kept telling people what they were doing up there – whatever that is. He said she freaked out and made a scene. Apparently she threatened to tell people he was doing sexual rites."

"You think he killed her to shut her up?"

"I do."

"Why did he dump her in front of my house?"

"You might not want to hear this, Ivy, but I think he's carrying a weird torch for you," Jack said. "I don't think he's ever gotten over you. That's why he's fixated on the fact that he thinks you've never gotten over him."

"That's so ridiculous."

"You are over him, right?"

Ivy made a face. "Don't insult me. I'm sorry I ever dated him. It makes me feel … dirty."

Without thinking, Jack reached up and brushed a strand of her hair away from her face, taking them both by surprise. "I'm sorry. I shouldn't have done that."

"Don't worry about it," Ivy said. "It was just an impulse."

He was having a lot of those these days. "I ... it was still uncalled for."

Ivy sighed, frustrated. "I think you're right."

"I'm sorry. I shouldn't have touched you."

"Not about that," she scoffed. "Don't be such a woman. I was talking about going home. I'm exhausted, and if I stay here much longer I'm going to be getting a few impulses of my own."

Jack couldn't help but grin. "You should definitely go then."

"Agreed." Ivy started moving toward the door. "If you get somewhere ... ?"

"I'll call you. I promise."

"I'll talk to you soon then."

TWO HOURS LATER CHAD WAS IN THE OFFICE TALKING TO HIS lawyer and Jack was sitting at his desk staring at the book. For lack of anything better to do, he typed the title into an Internet search engine and perused the items that came up.

Most of it was nonsense. There was a handful of people trying to use it as a weapon like Chad. Most of the talk was about how ridiculous the book was. Jack was about to give up when something caught his eye. He clicked on the link.

"What are you doing?" Brian asked, walking up behind Jack's desk with a mug of coffee in his hand.

"I searched for the book," Jack said. "I was just curious."

"Did you find something?"

"Actually, I did. Mona went to Central Michigan University, right?"

Brian nodded.

"Well, *The Covenant* was used as a textbook in a comparative religion class in the fall," Jack said. "That can't be a coincidence, right?"

"I don't know," Brian said, shrugging. "Ivy said it was fiction."

"I'm still going to call," Jack said. "Do you think it's too late?"

"It's not even dark yet," Brian said. "Knock yourself out."

It took Jack more than an hour to track down the professor he was looking for, and when he finally got the woman on the phone she was less than thrilled about being bugged on her private time. After profuse apologies, Amy Fowler finally agreed to answer his questions.

"I need to know how *The Covenant* became part of your curriculum," Jack said. "My understanding is that the book was originally meant as fiction."

"That's exactly why I used it," Amy said. "A very small group of people latched onto the book and purported it to be true. We were basically talking about how a fiction book could somehow be turned into non-fiction by a group of believers."

"Kind of like *The Blair Witch Project*?"

"In theory, yes," Amy said. "It was just a small part of the semester. We only talked about it for two classes."

"Was Mona Wheeler in your class?"

"I'll have to look it up on my laptop," Amy said. "I'll boot it up now. Do you have any other questions?"

"There's a lot of faux paganism in the book," Jack said. "Do you think people latched onto it because of that?"

"Maybe," Amy said. "The thing is, the book was written in the eighties. Most people ignored it then. It didn't become popular until the nineties."

"Why?"

"There was a paranormal resurgence in the nineties, and whenever that happens people devour everything they can get their hands on," Amy said. "That's what happened here. Okay, here's my class list. Hold on ... yes, Mona Wheeler was a student in my class during the fall semester."

"That's where she learned about *The Covenant*," Jack said. "The problem is, she should've known that it was fiction because of your class. Did she miss a lot of classes?"

"Um, hold on," Amy said. "I'm better with faces than names. Let me look up her student file."

"Did any of the students in your class express interest in following the book in reality?"

"No," Amy said. "Of course, they might not have made their interest public. I kind of ravaged the book. If they wanted a good grade, they were not going to admit to finding *The Covenant* feasible. Here we go … okay, I remember her."

"What can you tell me about her?"

"She was diligent," Amy said. "When the semester started, she was all wide-eyed and excited. I see students like her all the time. A lot of kids are here for the partying. She was here for the learning."

"Why do I sense a but?"

"Toward the end of the semester she became … distracted."

"Because of *The Covenant*?"

"I have no idea," Amy said. "If I had to guess, though, I would say it was a boy."

"Why do you say that?"

"Now that I know who she is, I can tell you that one other thing about Mona Wheeler stuck out to me," Amy said.

Jack waited.

"I had a TA for two semesters," Amy said. "He was extremely good for the first semester, and then he kind of fell off. He stopped turning in his assignments on time. Sometimes he wouldn't show up for work at all."

"What does this have to do with Mona Wheeler?"

"TAs grade papers at times, but I'm one of those professors who does spot checks," Amy said. "When I spot checked some of his work I found that I didn't have corresponding papers for the grades he was giving out."

"Meaning?"

"Meaning he was giving grades – good ones – for work that wasn't completed," Amy said. "Mona Wheeler was one of those students. She did supply papers after the fact, and I did pass her, but I had to let the TA go."

"Why would he pass people if they didn't turn in the work?"

"It's happened before," Amy said. "This was the first time it happened to me, but there was a scandal about two years back where a TA was being paid by a bunch of athletes to make sure they passed."

"Was this TA being paid?"

"Not like you might expect," Amy said. "We did an investigation, and it seems the students in my class were not paying with money."

"Were they all women?"

"How did you know?"

"Lucky guess," Jack said dryly. "What was this TA's name?"

"Heath Graham."

Jack froze, surprised. "Excuse me?"

"Heath Graham."

"How well did you know Heath?"

"Relatively well," Amy said. "Like I said, he was diligent in the beginning. It wasn't until the end that he seemed to fall apart."

"Does the name Chad Hamilton mean anything to you?"

"Should it?"

"He's this local ... quack ... we have up here," Jack explained. "He's built a whole compound around *The Covenant*. I was up there the other day. Heath Graham is one of his followers."

"Well, that makes sense," Amy said. "After the scandal, Heath was expelled from school."

"He was expelled and the students weren't?"

"Correct."

"When was the last time you saw him?"

"The day he was expelled," Amy said. "He was brought in front of the disciplinary committee and axed on the spot."

"How did he take it?"

"He was angry, but he was also ... resigned," Amy said. "I think he was expecting it. My understanding is that he packed up his belongings and left the campus that night. I guess we know where he ended up now."

"I guess so," Jack said, rubbing his chin. "I just have one more question. Did Heath ever seem susceptible to suggestion to you?"

"That's a hard question to answer," Amy said. "I'm in a position of power where he's concerned. He always did as I asked. I guess, in theory, I would have to say yes. Just how much suggestion are we talking about here?"

"The compound is full of mostly women," Jack said. "Other than Heath, I think I only saw two other men. I assumed he was at the compound because he was grandfathered in through his mother or something. I'm not sure that's the case, though."

"I wish you luck, detective," Amy said. "Religious manipulation is one of the few things that really gets me riled up."

"I can see that," Jack said. "Thank you for your time."

Brian was back at Jack's desk a few minutes after he disconnected. "Anything?"

"We have a whole lot of something," Jack said. "I ... what's going on with Hamilton's lawyer?"

"They're still in there talking."

"We need to get in there," Jack said. "I have a few questions about Heath Graham, and right now Hamilton is the only one who can answer them. Come on."

Twenty-Four

"Happy dinner, Nicodemus."

Ivy leaned over and stroked the cat's soft fur wearily. Although he often craved attention, when the dinner bell rang, Nicodemus considered it a solitary experience. He turned his back on Ivy and blocked her off from his dish – just in case she might want to steal some of it.

"Have fun, glutton."

Ivy left Nicodemus to his dinner and moved toward her library. A nice book and her favorite blanket sounded like the perfect way to unwind, she told herself. It had been days since she'd been able to relax. Now that Chad was in custody, she was safe.

So why did she feel so edgy?

Ivy selected a simple murder mystery from the shelf, knowing anything more taxing wouldn't sink in, and settled on the couch. She was only two pages in when she thought she heard something outside. She leaned forward, cocking her head to the side so she could listen closer. When she didn't hear anything again she returned her attention to the book. Living so close to the woods meant she had a lot of nocturnal visitors of the furry persuasion – most of which Nicodemus hunted from the window and terrorized until they moved a safe distance away. When he was done with his dinner, Ivy was sure he would scare whatever was scrounging around the front garden away with a few well-placed howls.

Ivy was just getting back into the flow of the book when she heard the noise again. This time it was accompanied by the sound of something rattling – and she was almost certain it was her garbage cans.

"That raccoon," Ivy grumbled, getting to her feet.

She stalked through the house, throwing open the door in an attempt to scare the scavenging raccoon away. He'd become a frequent guest, and Max was insisting on replacing her older bins with newer ones that had lids that fastened in such a way that a raccoon – no matter how industrious – couldn't get inside.

"Hey, bandit, there's nothing in there," Ivy said, narrowing her eyes so she could focus on the area where the trashcans were located. "You're going to be really disappointed when you tip that thing over."

When the bins clanged one more time, Ivy sighed and hopped off the porch, heading in the direction of the racket. She was almost upon the cans, ready to scare the creature physically with a loud yell, when she realized it was no animal rummaging through her garbage.

It was a man.

Ivy opened her mouth to scream, but it died on her lips when the man swiveled so he was facing her.

"HOW DID YOU MEET HEATH GRAHAM?" JACK ASKED, FOCUSING keenly on Chad as he conversed with his lawyer, Deacon Reynolds.

"My client is not going to answer that question," Reynolds said.

"Yes, he is," Jack said. "I want to know how Heath Graham became involved with your client, and I want to know now."

"May I ask why you're asking questions about Mr. Graham?" Reynolds asked.

"Because I found that this book was used in a comparative religion class at Central Michigan University," Jack replied, not seeing any reason to lie as he lifted the copy of *The Covenant* up for Chad and

Reynolds to see. "Heath Graham was a TA in that class, and he lied about paper grades for a number of students, including Mona Wheeler."

Chad balked. "Wait. What?"

"You didn't know Heath and Mona knew each other?"

"I knew they were acquainted, but I didn't know that," Chad said.

"Mr. Hamilton, please, let me handle this," Reynolds interrupted.

"Shut up," Jack said. "I'm not going to ask your client anything about his own activities right now. When I do, you can step in and speak for him. For now, I want to hear about Heath. How did he come to be a part of your compound?"

"He just showed up one day," Chad said. "I'm not sure how he heard about us, but he volunteered his services as my second in command."

"How did that go over?"

"I sent him away," Chad said. "I didn't want his ... sort ... at Covenant."

"Because he has a penis?"

"No," Chad scowled. "Because ... just bite me."

"When did you agree to let Heath join?"

"He kept coming around," Chad said. "One day I would find him helping the women in the field. The next day I would find him cleaning the living quarters. Finally, it just made sense to let him join. Once he told me he was gay, I didn't see what the harm in having him around was."

"Gay?"

"That's what he said. He never showed any interest in my women. Trust me. I was looking."

Jack made a face. "Heath was expelled from the university because of the cheating scandal," he said. "He only helped female students, and he wasn't doing it for money."

Chad faltered. "But ... he's gay."

"He's not," Jack said. "Tell me about Heath's interactions with Mona."

"I don't ... I never purposely sought them out to watch," Chad said, thoughtful. "I knew they were familiar with one another, but I thought it was just because they were passing acquaintances on campus. I honestly never saw anything to pique my suspicion."

"Did you know Heath was familiar with *The Covenant* before he came to the compound?"

"He was a true believer."

"He was part of a class where they ridiculed and mocked the book," Jack corrected. "I'm betting you didn't know that."

"But he said ... ."

"How did he find you? Mona was with your group first, right?"

"I met Mona at a fall festival in Bellaire in the fall," Chad said. "She seemed interested in our group, so I started ... talking ... to her whenever I got the chance. I invited her to a number of our public appearances."

"You mean you started to groom her," Jack corrected.

"I talked to her," Chad said.

"Did she let on that she knew *The Covenant* was fiction, too?"

Chad shifted uncomfortably. "I ... ."

"I don't care about your cult," Jack said. "I care about the murder. You said you didn't murder Mona. We have a second suspect now, although I'm not ruling you out. Tell me about Mona."

"She was really ... energetic at first," Chad said.

"You told me that."

"No, I mean she jumped right in and wanted to help," Chad said. "Frankly, she was more interested in hanging out with the women than me."

Jack stilled. "Wait a minute ... you said you had sex with her."

"I didn't say that."

"You insinuated it."

"I ... we never had occasion to consummate our promise."

"I thought you were the Promise?"

"I am."

"I don't understand," Jack said.

"That's because he's making it up as he goes along," Brian said. "Enough is enough here, Chad. You start volunteering information about Mona or I'm going to lock you up right now."

"You can't do that," Reynolds argued.

"Shut up," Brian snapped. "Start talking, Chad."

Chad sighed and ran his hand through his hair, frustrated. "I didn't know what Mona was doing when she first came to the compound," he said. "We talked a few times before she came for a tour. When she came for the tour, she was determined to be accepted into our group.

"She seemed really industrious and helpful," Chad said. "After the winter thaw, she started showing up every weekend. She would help in the fields, and she even volunteered to babysit. She would spend time with me, but she never seemed excited about it."

An idea was starting to form in Jack's mind. "She wasn't really a member of your group, was she?"

"No," Chad said. "I wasn't lying when I said I caught her telling people about what was going on at the compound. I found out, though, that she was doing it as part of a college assignment. She was trying to infiltrate us. She was undercover."

"For a college class?"

"She said it wasn't assigned, but if she could bring us down then she would have something to show some professor who thought she was a cheater," Chad said.

"You're starting to look like the guilty party again," Jack said.

"I didn't kill her," Chad said. "While I didn't like being fooled, I honestly didn't see how a college project could hurt us. Obviously Mona couldn't stay. That's why I banned her."

"What if she turned what she found into the police?"

"I'm not doing anything illegal," Chad said.

"Are you sure? There are rumors you're cultivating pot up there."

"Did you find any in your search?"

Jack shook his head. "That doesn't mean you're not hiding it somewhere else. It's a big area."

"I'll call the state police," Brian said. "They have more resources. They can have dogs up there and search the surrounding area within a few hours."

"Wait!" Chad held up his hands, desperate. "I ... ."

"Don't say another word," Reynolds said.

"Yeah, don't say another word," Jack said. "Let me fill the rest of this in for you and your attorney. Heath didn't join because he was a believer. He joined because he blamed Mona for being expelled. He got expelled and she got a second chance. He was bitter. When he got up there, he realized there was potential for making money.

"If Mona turned everything she found over to her professor that would put all of you at risk," Jack said. "Heath didn't want to lose money and stature to Mona. Not again. He wanted her to pay, and when you banned her, he realized he was going to lose that chance."

"Heath didn't even know about the pot," Chad scoffed, immediately realizing what he'd said. "I mean ... crap."

"Yeah, crap," Jack said. "Heath murdered Mona to shut her up. I'm not sure why he dumped her here, but I'll be sure to ask him when we take him into custody. He wasn't up at the compound when we searched it earlier. Where is he?"

"I haven't seen him since we came over here to shop for trees the other day," Chad said. "I sent him away so I could talk to Ivy alone, and I haven't seen him since. He wasn't in the parking lot when I left, so I assumed he would find another ride back."

Jack shifted sharply. "What do you mean? Heath was in town with you the day you went after Ivy at the nursery?"

"I didn't go after her."

"I will beat you," Jack snapped, his heart fluttering.

"He was with me," Chad said, making a face. "I haven't seen him since, though."

Jack jumped to his feet and strode toward the office door.

"Where are you going?" Brian asked, confused.

"Heath Graham was here the day someone left a threat for Ivy on her front porch," Jack said. "He was ... enamored ... with her when we were up at the compound that first day. He's the one who killed Mona Wheeler."

"I ... do you think he's going after Ivy?"

"Of course he's going after Ivy," Jack said. "Why else would he leave the message? I have to call her."

"What are you going to tell her?"

"To stay in her house," Jack said. "You call Max and get him over there right away. She needs a wall of protection so Heath doesn't approach her."

"What if it's too late?"

Jack was grim. "Then I'll kill him."

Twenty-Five

"Max! What are you doing here? You scared the life out of me."

Ivy held her hand to her heart as she tried to catch her breath. When she first saw the figure moving by the trashcans, her mind went to a scary place. Now she was just angry. Her brother picked the oddest times to show up and irritate her.

"I came to make sure you were okay," Max said, making a face. "I saw something by your trashcans when I came up. I got distracted. You really need new cans. That raccoon is never going to leave if it knows you put out a buffet for it every night."

"You scared me!"

"I'm sorry," Max said, moving forward and giving Ivy a brief hug. "I actually came here because I wanted to make sure you were safe. I heard about the threatening flowers, by the way. I can't tell you how great it is to hear about it from someone else. It made my day."

"How did you hear about it?"

"I played basketball with Sean Nixon up at the high school this afternoon. He told me."

"Brian has a big mouth," Ivy grumbled.

"I also heard that Jack Harker spent the night here to protect you," Max said, lifting his eyebrows. "Is that part of the story true, too? Are you two ... ?" Max made a suggestive motion with his hand.

"No," Ivy said, glaring at him. "He slept on the couch. Stop being ... you."

"Did you want him to sleep somewhere else?"

"Max!"

"You like him," Max said, refusing to back down. "Don't deny it. I see it when you look at him. There's no shame in it. You're an adult, after all. You're allowed to like a guy."

Ivy pinched the bridge of her nose, too tired to keep up the fight. "I do like him."

"I know. He likes you, too. He can't take his eyes off of you when you're in a room together."

"He doesn't want anything," Ivy said, her voice small. "He's dealing with other stuff. He doesn't have anything to give. He's already told me that."

"That was a little forward of him," Max grumbled.

"He was honest," Ivy said. "I admire him for it. I don't want anything either."

"You want him," Max countered. "You just admitted it. Don't take it back now. We're finally getting somewhere."

"Even if I do want him, and I'm not saying I do, but if I did want to try and see if we could have something, he's not ready," Ivy said. "Trust me. He's dealing with other stuff. I'm not a consideration for him."

"You seem upset about that."

"I ... there's something about him," Ivy said. "I can't explain it. It's like he *calls* to me."

"I think it might have something to do with the fact that he's tall, built, and looks like a Greek god."

Ivy smirked. "He's handsome," she said. "It's not just that, though. There's something else there."

"Have you considered telling him this?"

"No."

"Why? Ivy, I love you. You owe yourself a chance for some happiness. If this is the guy who can give it to you, don't you at least want to give it a try?"

"No," Ivy said, her eyes serious. "I would never try to force a situation that he didn't want, and he doesn't want this. I'm not an idiot. I know he's attracted to me. He's pretty much admitted it.

"He's also admitted that he can't deal with a relationship right now," she continued. "I'm not sure what drove him out of Detroit, but I know it was terrible. Until he deals with that, there's no room for anything else on his plate.

"It's sad. It's a little depressing. It's honest, though," Ivy said. "I have nothing but respect for him. He's not trying to play games. He's not trying to hurt me. In the grand scheme of things, he's really trying to protect us both."

"That's very pragmatic," Max said, rolling his eyes. "You have one little problem, though."

Ivy waited.

"When your heart gets involved, the best-laid plans fall by the wayside," Max said. "You can't stay away from him, and he can't stay away from you."

"That's only because of this case," Ivy said. "It's almost over. Chad is in custody."

"I'm relieved for that," Max said. "I'm still willing to wager that Jack finds a way to cross paths with you even when this case is over with."

"Do you want to bet?"

"I think that's what a wager is," Max said.

Ivy extended her hand. "Fine. Fifty bucks says that once this case is over with Jack Harker is going to find every excuse in the book to stay away from me."

Max shook her hand. "Done. When I'm right, I want my fifty bucks in the form of that lilac lotion you make every June."

Ivy's eyebrows flew up. "What? Why?"

"The women love it, and they love me when I have it."

"You really are a pig."

"I try," Max said. "Now, why don't you go inside and fix me something to eat? I'll make sure these cans are secured and then I'll be inside."

"You're staying?"

"You're my sister," Max said. "You've been threatened. It's my job to stay."

"I told you Chad was in custody."

"Well, until he's charged or admits he's guilty, I'm your new shadow."

"You can't be my shadow," Ivy said.

"Why not?"

"If you're supposed to be my shadow, I'm going to have to go on a diet," she said, smirking. "You make me look hippy."

Max pointed at the door. "You'd better make me an awesome dinner – and I am not hippy!"

"SHE'S NOT PICKING UP HER PHONE," JACK SAID, FRUSTRATED. "Why wouldn't she pick up her phone?"

Brian extended his hands, palms up. "Maybe she can't hear it."

"That cottage is minuscule," Jack said, pacing. "There's nowhere inside that she couldn't hear her phone."

"Maybe she's outside."

Jack balked. "Why would she be outside? I told her to stay inside."

"Yes, but she's a woman," Brian said. "They do what they want when they want. It's part of their genetic makeup. They can't help themselves."

"Did you get Max?"

"I left a message on his cell phone," Brian said, his face reflecting the helplessness he was feeling. "Maybe they're together."

"Maybe they're not," Jack snapped, turning on his heel and stalking toward the door.

"Where are you going?"

"To find her," Jack said. "She's in trouble. I can just ... feel it."

· · ·

IVY RUMMAGED AROUND THE REFRIGERATOR FOR A FEW minutes, ultimately settling on fresh vegetables and rice. She wasn't going to go out of her way and cook a feast for Max. That would just be rewarding him for bad behavior.

Her mind was busy with cooking for the next few minutes, but after a few minutes she realized Max was still outside. He was probably trying to entice the raccoon closer so he could catch it. That would be just like him.

She moved to the door and opened it, stepping out onto the front porch and searching the area by the trashcans for her brother.

"Max? Are you coming in or not? I'm not just cooking for me. You demanded dinner. You're going to eat it."

He didn't answer, but Ivy heard shuffling on the far side of the house.

"You're such a pain," she grumbled, padding down the steps in her bare feet and peering around the edge of the house. "Max, what are you doing?"

The figure standing there wasn't Max, and it took Ivy a moment to realize what she was seeing. Her big, strong brother was lying prone on the ground. He wasn't moving, and from her vantage point, Ivy couldn't ascertain if he was breathing.

The figure standing over him was holding a large hunting knife, the serrated edges gleaming under the moonlight. There was no blood on it, which was a mild relief, but Ivy realized she was in a load of trouble when she recognized the figure.

"Heath."

"Hello, Ivy," Heath said, smiling evilly. "I can't tell you how much I've been looking forward to our little ... tête-à-tête."

"Nice phrase," Ivy said, fighting to keep her face neutral and her breathing regular as she tried to figure a way out of the situation. "Did you kill my brother?"

"Not yet," Heath said. "I was disappointed when he showed up. I thought he was going to ruin our evening. Then he saw some raccoon and started following it. It gave me the opportunity to come up behind him without him noticing. He's just knocked out."

"That's good," Ivy said. "It wouldn't be a very nice start to our … date … if you killed my brother."

"Oh, I'm going to kill him," Heath said. "I just haven't gotten around to it yet. I was hoping you would stay inside for a little bit longer. I was just getting around to my art project."

Ivy shuddered, knowing full well what he meant by that. "Leave Max alone," Ivy said. "You're here for me. He has nothing to do with this."

"He's still an obstacle," Heath said. "He's standing between you and me … and our happily ever after."

"He's not an obstacle," Ivy said. "You said you came up behind him. He didn't see you. He doesn't even know who you are. Please … leave Max alone. You're here for me."

"I am here for you," Heath said, tilting his head to the side as he regarded Ivy. "Did you like my flowers?"

"They were nice."

"They have certain … properties."

"I know," Ivy said. "I run a nursery. I know how to recognize flowers."

"I guess I didn't take that into consideration," Heath said. "You didn't even pick them up."

"That's because I knew they were dangerous."

"Did you like the card?"

"It was very … expressive," Ivy said. "Have you been here watching me all this time?"

"Chad left me when you called his manhood into question at the nursery," Heath said. "That was funny, by the way. He deserves to be taken down a peg or two. He's got some ego issues."

Ivy didn't think Chad was the only one with ego issues. "I don't understand any of this. Why did you kill Mona?"

"I knew Mona from school," Heath explained. "She suckered me into giving her passing grades on papers when she didn't turn them in. She pretended to like me. She said we were going to go on a date.

"Then, when we got caught, she turned on me," he continued. "She told the board that I pressured her and was demanding sex. She got off with probation and I got expelled."

"That must have been hard for you." Ivy had no idea what to do but keeping Heath talking – instead of carving – seemed like a viable option.

"It wasn't fair," Heath said. "I was one year away from graduating. Now I never can."

"You could go to another school."

"I don't want to go to another school," Heath said. "It's not my fault Mona was a slut."

"Why did Mona go to the compound? Do you know?"

"At first I thought she was a believer," Heath said. "I watched her for a few weeks after I was expelled. Every weekend she drove up to that compound. I watched her there – from the exact spot you were hiding the other day – and then I realized she wasn't a believer at all."

"What do you mean?"

"She was trying to bolster her position at the college," Heath said. "She thought, if she could bring Chad's compound down, she would be able to impress Professor Fowler. She thought she might even win some awards.

"After watching the compound, I realized I had a place there," he continued. "I approached Chad, but he wanted all the women for himself. I didn't care about the women. The only woman I cared about was Mona."

"Because she had to pay?"

"Of course she had to pay," Heath said. "She ruined my life – and she didn't follow through with her promise. She didn't go out with me. So I told Chad I was gay and he let me in. He thought it was a great idea as long as I didn't move in on his women. That was pretty easy.

"You should've seen Mona's face when she came up for the next weekend and saw me there," he said. "She was freaking out. She had no idea what to do."

"Why didn't she tell Chad what you were doing?"

"The same reason I didn't tell Chad what she was doing," Heath said. "We were both working him."

"Why did you kill Mona?"

"Because she had it coming."

"But ... you worked together for weeks," Ivy said. "What happened to make you ... do what you did?"

"Chad found out what Mona was up to," Heath replied. "I tried to tell him that she was dangerous, but he wouldn't listen. Instead of dealing with her the way he should've, he banished her.

"He didn't think a college class project would be enough to bring him down," he continued. "Of course, he didn't think anyone but his chosen few knew about the pot field he was growing on the adjacent piece of land."

"I knew he was hiding something up there," Ivy grumbled.

"He's nowhere near as smart as he thinks he is," Heath agreed. "So I let him banish her. Then, when she was getting ready to leave, I took things into my own hands. She didn't even see it coming.

"When I approached her, she thought I was there to gloat," he said. "That changed pretty quickly when she saw the knife."

"And no one saw you?"

"Nope."

"Why did you carve the symbols into her body?"

"At first I planned on framing Chad," Heath said. "I thought the symbols would lead the cops right to him, which they did. The problem I had was that I never took into consideration that the cops would probably search the woods surrounding the compound. I didn't realize that until Mona was already dead.

"There was no way I could take over the entire operation if there was no operation to take over," he said. "That's when I knew I had to come up with a different solution."

"Why did you dump her in my yard?"

"Oh, you can thank Chad for that," Heath said. "He was always talking about you. Ivy Morgan, the one who got away. I thought he was just babbling like an idiot until he mentioned you were a witch."

Realization dawned on Ivy. "You thought the police would assume that since I'm a witch, I murdered her as some sort of ritual."

"Isn't that what witches do?"

"No."

"That was another miscalculation on my part," Heath said. "I guess I'm off my game. I have been ever since Mona ruined my life. You're the last piece of the puzzle, though. Once I kill you, then everything will be fixed. Covenant will be mine."

"How do you figure that?"

"The cops will know that Chad killed both of you," Heath said. "This will be the final nail in his coffin. If it's any consolation, I am sorry it came to this. I just … I need Chad to go away. I need all of this to go away."

"I see," Ivy said, racking her brain. She knew she was out of time. "You do realize the cops have Chad down at the station right now, right?"

Heath balked. "What? No, they don't."

"They do," Ivy said. "I was down there earlier. If you'd been listening closer when Max and I were outside talking you would've realized that."

"I think you're lying," Heath said. "This is the only way you can figure to get yourself out of this situation."

"Not the only way," Ivy said, making her decision quickly. She turned on her heel and bolted – not toward the house, but toward the woods she knew better than anyone else. She knew she had to draw Heath away from Max, and this was the best way she could figure to do it. The only way they were both going to survive was for Ivy to lead Heath into a world he didn't recognize.

He was on her turf now.

"Ivy!"

Twenty-Six

"What is that smell?" Brian asked, wrinkling his nose as he looked into Ivy's kitchen.

The door to the cottage was open when they arrived, and Jack took the steps two at a time as he raced into the house. He found the cat sitting in the middle of the room, a disturbed look on his face, and the cottage was filled with a thin film of smoke.

A skillet sat on the stove, the flame on, but whatever was inside was burnt beyond recognition. Jack turned the stove off and dumped the skillet into the sink before turning swiftly. "Where is she?"

"I don't think the cat can answer you," Brian said.

"Something happened to her," Jack said. "Heath was here."

"You don't know that."

"I do know that," Jack seethed, moving back toward the door. "Where would he have taken her?"

"We don't know she's been taken anywhere," Brian said, following Jack out onto the porch. "I … now where are you going?"

Jack moved around the front of the house, staring into the trees and cocking his head to the side to see if he could hear anything. Out of the corner of his eye, he saw something lying on the ground next to the house. He started toward the figure, his heart dropping. *Was Ivy already gone?*

"Call for an ambulance!"

"What is it," Brian asked, appearing behind him. "I ... crap. Max."

Jack knelt down next to the fallen figure, pressing his fingers to the side of Max's neck and hoping beyond hope the amiable man was alive. The second Jack touched him Max stirred, his fingers shooting out and grabbing him tightly around the wrist.

"Max? It's Jack. You're okay. What happened?"

"I'm not sure," Max said, rubbing the back of his head. "I ... Ivy. Where is Ivy?"

"We don't know," Jack said, his eyes serious. "What do you remember?"

"We were outside talking," Max said. "The raccoon was in the garbage again. I ... she went in to make dinner. I saw the raccoon and I decided to follow it and ... that's it. The lights went out."

"Did you see who it was?"

"No," Max said, struggling to a sitting position and cringing as he reached around to the back of his head. "Where's Ivy?"

"We'll find her," Jack said. "I ... what time did you get here?"

"A little after seven. What time is it?"

"About twenty after," Jack said. "That means she hasn't been gone long."

"No more than ten minutes," Max said. "We talked for a few minutes. I told her to make me dinner and made fun of her because of ... well ... you."

"We'll have that discussion later," Jack said. "Did you hear a car?"

"There was no car," Max said.

"Where is your truck?"

"I parked at the nursery and walked over. I needed a potted plant. I have a date tomorrow, and women like plants."

Jack forced a grim smile for Max's benefit. "If he didn't have a car, that means they're in the woods. Maybe Ivy ran. Maybe she got away. Where would she go?"

"She'd only go one place," Max said. "It's where she feels safest."

"The fairy ring," Jack said, straightening. "Stay here. Brian is calling for help."

"Where are you going?"

"After her."

IVY WAS IN SHAPE. SHE KNEW HOW TO PACE HERSELF. SHE ALSO knew every indentation and rock outcropping in the area. There was no way Heath could take her by surprise. Not here.

That didn't make her safe, though. The woods were deep, but they didn't last forever. Ivy had no idea how long Heath would keep up his pursuit. And, if he gave up, would he return to her house and finish Max off? She couldn't let that happen.

Ivy slowed her pace. "Heath?"

"I'm coming for you, Ivy." His voice was behind her and to the right. He was close, but not close enough to touch her. Not yet. "You can't outrun me."

"I run all the time," Ivy said. "I run through these woods. I have the upper hand out here."

"You're still just a woman."

"And you have a problem with women, don't you?" An idea popped into Ivy's head. "You think women are beneath you. The problem is they keep outsmarting you. That's what really has you upset."

"No one has outsmarted me," Heath snapped.

He was closer, so Ivy changed her trajectory. She was taking him in the direction of the fairy ring, but she wanted to make sure she approached in the right spot.

"Mona outsmarted you," Ivy said, moving between two trees and ducking down so she could grab a fallen branch. "Mona had enough information to bring down you and Chad in one fell swoop."

"And where is Mona now?"

"Mona is gone, but she still brought you down," Ivy said. "Chad is in custody. I wasn't lying about that. Everyone is going to know you're guilty now. You're never going to inherit Chad's kingdom."

"Stop lying!"

LILY HARPER HART

Ivy slipped behind a large tree, pressing her back against the rough bark as she waited. One more push should propel him to the spot she wanted.

"I'm not lying," she said. "Do you want to know what my favorite thing about this whole situation is? You're going to be very popular in prison. You've got a pretty mouth, and lifers love a pretty mouth."

"I'm going to kill you!"

Ivy's heart was racing, and she squeezed her eyes shut when she heard Heath approaching. She was only going to get one shot at this.

"I'm going to give you something to do with your mouth in a second, Ivy," Heath said, panting. He was close now. Ivy could see him, but he didn't see her. "I'm going to rip you apart. You're going to be crying for your precious cop when I'm done with you. Then, right when you're begging me to kill you, I'm going to hurt you some more … just because I can."

"I doubt it," Ivy said, stepping up and taking aim. She swung the heavy tree branch with as much force as she could muster, making contact with the side of Heath's head. The sound was sickening, but Ivy didn't relent. As Heath listed to the side, confused, she slammed the branch into his head a second time.

"Oomph." Heath dropped to one knee, fighting to stay upright even though his body was telling him it might not be an option. "You, bitch," he hissed.

Ivy lashed out with her foot, catching him under his chin and knocking him to his side. He landed hard, his face bouncing off the green underbrush.

Ivy had seen enough horror movies to know that even though Heath looked like he was down, that didn't mean he was done. She took a step back, keeping her eyes on him as she brandished the branch again. Part of her wanted him to die here. The other part of her knew that would do nothing but taint her favorite place.

The sound of footsteps in the thick trees drew Ivy's attention, and when Jack burst into the clearing with his gun drawn, she almost wept in relief. "Jack."

"Thank God," Jack said. "I … are you okay?"

Ivy nodded, biting her lower lip in an effort to stave off the tears.

190

"Are you going to cry?"

"No." Her voice came out in a squeak.

"Come here, honey," Jack said, gesturing toward her.

Ivy did as instructed, giving Heath a wide berth as she shuffled her way to Jack. The second she was within touching distance he swept her against his broad chest with one arm while he kept his gun trained on Heath with the other. "You can cry now, honey. I won't tell anyone."

The feeling of Jack's strong heart beating against her check was all Ivy could take. She burst into tears, letting Jack stroke the back of her head as he whispered quiet words to soothe her. It was over. She was safe. The only thing left at risk was her heart, and right now she couldn't muster the energy to care.

"MAX!"

Ivy broke into a run when she saw her brother sitting on the bottom step of her porch. He was on his feet, enveloping her in his own hug, within seconds. "You scared me, pop tart."

"Don't call me that," Ivy growled.

Max tilted her face back so he could study it, the unmistakable sign of dried tears on her cheeks throwing him. "Did he … ?"

"He never got his hands on me," Ivy said, her voice cracking. "I … I left you here. I made him chase me into the woods. I didn't know what else to do."

"Do you think I'm going to be mad at you for keeping us both alive?" Now Max was the one struggling to hold back tears. "You saved us both, pop tart."

"Don't call me that."

"Okay." Max pressed a kiss to the top of her head. "Where is Jack?"

"He's coming," Ivy said. "I hit Heath with a tree branch a couple of times. Then I kicked him. He … um … landed in a specific spot."

"What does that mean?" Brian asked, alarmed. "Is he seriously hurt?"

"Not in the strictest sense of the word."

"I need you to be more specific, Ivy," Brian said. "What exactly is going on?"

Jack picked that moment to shove Heath out of the woods in front of him. The second Brian saw Heath, his mouth tipped up at the corners. "Is that … ?"

"I remembered where the Poison Ivy was and purposely knocked him down there," Ivy said. "I thought he deserved it."

"Why does Jack look so upset?"

"I forgot to tell him what Heath was on before he cuffed him," Ivy replied, her expression rueful. "It's all over his hands again."

Max barked out a hoarse laugh, slinging an arm around Ivy's shoulders as he watched Jack lead Heath to the waiting police car. "Do you have any lotion left?"

"I made some more after he took the last bottle. I feel kind of bad. He ran after me and now … ."

"He'll survive, Ivy," Max said. "He was a lot more worried about you than the Poison Ivy."

"It's still my fault. It's happened twice."

"Go get the lotion," Max said. "He looks miserable."

By the time Ivy came back, Heath was leaning against the car and he was screaming about the "fire of a thousand suns" burning his skin. Ivy kept her lips pressed firmly together as Jack extended his hands and watched her squirt the lotion onto them. He rubbed his hands together, sighing as the lotion did its work and relieved the itchiness. All the while he never took his eyes off of Ivy's face.

"Are you okay?"

"I'm fine," Ivy said. "I … are you okay? I'm so sorry this happened. Again."

"You don't look sorry," Jack said. "You look like you're trying to keep yourself from laughing."

"That's a horrible thing to say. I … ." When Ivy lifted her eyes to meet Jack's she saw he was the one grinning. "You're messing with me."

"Oh, honey, I wouldn't ever mess with you."

The term of endearment tugged on her heart. It also brought her back to reality. "I guess I'll be seeing less of you now that this is over."

"I guess," Jack said, his voice low.

"That's probably best," Ivy said. "There will be fewer … impulses."

"Yeah," Jack agreed, his expression wistful. "I meant everything I said. I don't have anything to give you. I really wish I did, though. I just … you deserve more."

"I don't expect anything from you," Ivy said. "You went above and beyond tonight. You … saved me."

"You saved yourself," Jack countered. "You beat him. I just transported him."

"I'll leave the lotion here," Ivy said, taking a step back. The glassy sheen of her eyes was almost enough to bring Jack to his knees. "Put it on as often as you can."

"I will. Thank you."

"What about me?" Heath whined.

"You can suffer," Ivy said, moving away from Jack without another glance. She squared her shoulders and headed toward the house. "I'll find something to feed you, Max."

Max watched her walk into the house, and when she disappeared, he turned his attention to Jack.

"That was disappointing," Brian said, following Max's gaze. "I thought for sure there would be some kissing or something."

"Don't worry about it," Max said. "They're nowhere near being done."

"How can you know that?"

"Because they've spent time together now," Max said. "They'll be miserable without one another." He clapped Brian on the shoulder. "There are just some things you can't fight."

"And you think this is one of those things?"

"I know it is," Max said. "Take care of him. He looks morose. I'll go handle my sister. Fifty bucks says they can't go a week without seeing each other."

"You want to bet on your sister's love life? That's low."

"A hundred bucks?"

"You're on."

Twenty-Seven

J ack studied Ivy through his windshield, watching as she
stretched on the grass next to the basketball court. She was
getting ready to go on a run, but he had different ideas.

They weren't good ones. He knew that. Three days without
seeing Ivy was all he could take, though. He was opening a door here.
Odds were that neither of them would be stepping through it today –
but it was still a step.

He just wanted to see her smile.

Ivy lifted her head when she heard a door slam shut, her heart
rolling with pleasure when she saw Jack striding toward her. He was
clearly off duty if the shorts and T-shirt were any indications. He also
had a basketball in his hand and a challenging look on his face.

"What are you doing here?"

"I came to shoot a few hoops," Jack said. It was a lie – but only a
little one. "I didn't know you would be here."

Ivy narrowed her eyes, suspicious. She wasn't sure she believed
him. "You're going to shoot hoops alone?"

"No," Jack said. "You're going to shoot them with me. I believe we
have an outstanding bet. That's what we decided, right?"

"It is," Ivy hedged. "I just ... are you sure you want to do this?"

Her meaning was clear.

"We're just playing basketball right now," Jack said, serious. "I kind of thought we could shoot for a little bit, talk, and just … hang out."

Ivy tilted her head to the side, considering. *Was that enough?* She decided quickly. It was enough for now. This would give them a chance to get to know one another without too much pressure. "What do I get if I win?"

"I thought you wanted me to weed your garden?"

"I do," Ivy said, hopping from the grass to the pavement. "I hate weeding."

"What do I get if I win?"

"I'll do all your landscaping for you," Ivy replied, not missing a beat.

Jack arched an eyebrow. "You will?"

"I have good taste. You're going to need me."

Jack grinned and bounced the ball to her. "You go first."

"I'm warning you that I'm really good."

"So you've told me," Jack said. "Shoot."

Ivy lifted the ball and threw it up from beyond the three-point line, smiling as it swished through the net without touching the rim. "See."

"I guess I shouldn't be surprised," Jack said, chuckling as he retrieved the ball. "You're good at everything you do."

"I am," Ivy agreed. "Tell me about Heath. What's going on there?"

"He confessed," Jack replied. "He says God made him do it, though, so he's clearly going to try and use insanity as a defense."

"Will that work?"

"Not likely," Jack said. "This will take months – years maybe – to wind through the courts. You know you're going to have to testify, right?"

"I figured. I'll be fine. I'm strong."

"You're definitely strong," Jack said, lining up his own shot and letting the ball go. He grimaced when it rimmed away.

"That's an H," Ivy said, jogging over to retrieve the ball before moving to the right side and drilling another shot.

Jack scowled. "I think you have home court advantage."

"Stop your whining," Ivy chided, retrieving her own ball and handing it to him. "Tell me about Chad."

"That's been shifted over to the state police," Jack said, eyeing the rim and throwing up the ball. "Son of a … ."

"That's an O."

"Thank you, Ivy," Jack said. "Anyway, Chad is in custody and the state police found the pot field. There are some human services groups working on finding a place for all the women to live."

"What's going to happen to the compound?"

"I have no idea."

Ivy moved to the free throw line and turned so her back was to the hoop. She used both hands to flip the ball over her shoulder, and when it swished through the net again Jack's heart sank. He had a feeling he was going to be weeding her garden – although the idea wasn't altogether unwelcome. "You're unbelievable."

"I try," Ivy said, smiling sweetly. "Your turn."

Jack grimaced. He knew there was no way he was going to make the shot, but he believed in being a good sport. He took up his position and tossed the ball over his shoulder. It was so wide it missed the backboard.

"That's an R."

"It's an N," Jack corrected.

"We're playing Horse," Ivy said.

"No, we're not," Jack said, grinning. "We're playing Honey. Something tells me I've already lost."

Ivy arched an eyebrow. "You don't know that. Somewhere down the line, you might think you've won."

"I'm looking forward to that," Jack said.

It didn't surprise him to find that he honestly was looking forward to it. For now, baby steps were enough, though.

CPSIA information can be obtained
at www.ICGtesting.com
Printed in the USA
BVHW031843270121
598911BV00015B/124